her SECRET

Malone Brothers Book 1

SAMANTHA COLE

Her Secret
(Former title: *Take the Money and Run*)

Copyright ©2016 Samantha A. Cole
All Rights Reserved.
Suspenseful Seduction Publishing

Her Secret is a work of fiction. Names, characters, businesses, organizations, places, events, and incidents either are the product of the author's imagination or are used fictitiously. Any resemblance to actual persons, living or dead, events, or locales is entirely coincidental.

Edited by Eve Arroyo
Cover by Samantha Cole

This story was originally written by Samantha Cole under a different pen name. It has been rewritten and rereleased.

Acknowledgements

As always, I have a list of people I need to thank:

My mom, for reading this story (without the cursing and steamier sex scenes) and encouraging me to start a new career in storytelling.

My beta readers, Jessica, Julie, Debbie, and Felisha, for convincing me this story could be resurrected from its earlier mess.

My editor, Eve Arroyo, for putting up with my comma handicap and making some great suggestions in order to get the book just right.

My Sexy Six-Pack Facebook group, for all your comments and encouragement which keeps me pecking away at my keyboard.

And last, but absolutely not least, my readers. It is because of you that I have a new career I truly love.

As always, to my friends and family.

Chapter 1

Through the convenience store window, Moriah Jensen eyed the black Escalade with Illinois plates rolling down the dinky little town's Main Street. Tugging on her baseball cap, she made sure her face was concealed as she hid behind the magazine rack to the left of the front door. The driver and the two passengers of the vehicle had their windows down as they swiveled their heads in every direction. It was obvious they were looking for someone . . . well, not just anyone—they were looking for her.

Shit. How had they found her again? She was in the middle of Ohio, in some town too tiny for its own Walmart. It was far from being the bustling metropolis Chicago was. How could they have picked this town, of all places, to look for her? This couldn't be happening. She'd been so careful, staying under the radar by using an alias and not using her ATM card. She'd picked a name similar to her own, Maura Jennings, so she wouldn't slip up and not respond to the fictional name.

Her driver's license! *Fuck!* She had given her real driver's license to the police officer yesterday when the college girls, who'd given her a lift, had gotten into a fender-bender on the way into town. Moriah hadn't been able to run from the scene because it happened right in front of a patrol car. After the officer had returned her license, she'd been allowed to leave, and she thought that was the end of it. But it must be how the men in the Escalade found her.

Damn it! She had to be more diligent, and at the first opportunity, she'd have to figure out how to get a forged license with her alias on it . . . something which could pass a cop's inspection. It would be better if she didn't get pulled over at all, but shit happened. And mistakes like that could get her arrested or, even worse, killed.

She glanced around the store, grateful to see no one was paying any attention to her. In her jeans and bland T-shirt, she wasn't wearing anything which would make her stand out. Hopefully, no one would remember seeing her if the men came in here asking questions. Hiking the strap of her large duffel bag higher on her shoulder, she watched the vehicle turn left at a traffic light two blocks down. When it was out of sight, she pulled her hat down further, exited the store, and hurried across the parking lot in the opposite direction.

The duffel and her backpack felt heavier with every step, and they prevented her from running as fast as she wanted to. But she couldn't leave either one behind—she needed the money, gun, and what few clothes she'd grabbed on her way out of Chicago.

The girls she'd gotten a lift from while hitchhiking had dropped her off last night at an old motel a few blocks away. With the bus station nearby, it was perfect for her to rest before getting a ticket to someplace far away from here . . . and Chicago. She headed in that direction now, and not wanting to be seen, she stayed behind the buildings and anything else which would conceal her. Her heart pounded in her chest every time she had to be in the open, and she prayed she would make it out of this bum-fuck town alive. She knew those men would have no problem killing her to get what they wanted.

Twenty minutes later, Moriah was huddled in the back of a bus heading to Pittsburgh, Pennsylvania, and from there, she would get another ticket to God-only-knew-where. As long as it was taking her far away, she didn't care. She had nothing left to care about—nothing except her own life.

Inching forward in silence, with his face painted tan and dark brown, the same colors of his camouflage fatigues, the man was almost invisible in the terrain surrounding a small village south of Mosul, Iraq. United States Navy Lieutenant KC Malone lay a mere forty yards behind a dilapidated structure where two U.S. Army pilots were being held captive. The building, a little larger than a tiki hut, was one of eight still standing in the otherwise destroyed and abandoned village, which was now occupied by ISIS forces. The men had been taken hostage after their AH-64 Apache helicopter had been shot down six weeks ago, but their current location was far from the crash site as they'd been moved by rebel forces several times. However, less than thirty-six hours ago, CIA intelligence had finally been able to pinpoint their position. Members of SEAL Team Six were being sent in to retrieve the men before they were moved again or killed in retribution for the recent slaying of a high-ranking ISIS leader.

It was two minutes before oh-four-hundred hours, and the entire camp of twenty-three terrorists was asleep, except for three guards who looked as if they desperately wanted to join their comrades. KC and his team had parachuted down to a landing zone approximately three miles away and had approached the village in stealth. They'd been in hiding for the past two hours, waiting for the guards to succumb to early morning fatigue and begin dozing off. The other fifteen members of the team were strategically spread out, surrounding the village, and awaiting KC's go-ahead order. Chief Tobias Anderson III was on his left, ready to recover the hostages with him. The rest of the team would provide cover and distractions. A support team was two minutes out by chopper if shit went south. The original Blackhawk helicopter also remained nearby, waiting to swoop down for extraction of the team with their recovered charges.

KC scanned the area one last time through his night vision goggles, checked the time, and then tapped the microphone on his communication headset. "It's a go."

He had to keep himself from chuckling when he heard a soft voice respond through his earpiece. "Here comes trouble!"

A half second later, an ammunition storage shack on the far side of the camp exploded in a thundering wall of flames. The terrorists, known in military speak as tangos, poured out into the compound in confusion and dropped to the ground as automatic gunfire was sprayed in their direction from all sides. KC and his chief quickly reached the back of the building housing the hostages and snuck their way around to the front entrance.

The ISIS rebels desperately tried to return fire at the invisible enemy well hidden in the dark of night. Those who were still alive were too busy running for cover to notice the two men entering the simple wood and brick structure. KC hurried over to the nearest man lying prone on the ground. Although the pilot was covered in dirt and grime, the lieutenant could still distinguish the remnants of the U.S. Army flight suit. The man appeared weak but alert. "Captain Nichols?" When the man nodded, his eyes widening in disbelief and hope, the SEAL continued with wry humor. "U.S. Navy, here to save your sorry fucking asses, sir. Are you able to run?"

The emaciated Captain nodded his head again and scrambled to his bare feet with the help of his rescuer. "I think so."

"Where's Lieutenant Fisher?"

"Over there," Nichols replied, indicating the southwest corner of the dirt floor. "He was beaten up pretty badly yesterday. Been in and out of it all night."

KC reached behind him, where he had a pair of combat boots and black socks hooked to his belt, and handed them to Nichols. "Here, quick. Throw these on. Figured you'd need them. I brought a pair for Fischer, but I doubt he'll be running."

Rushing over to the unconscious man lying near the back wall, KC did a quick assessment. He thanked God when he found the man was breathing and had a weak pulse. Unable to rouse the young pilot, he picked him up and threw him over his shoulder in a fireman's carry as if he were a five-pound sack of potatoes. He indicated for Nichols to join Chief Anderson where the big man stood at the door, his eyes and weapon aimed outside, providing cover. Speaking into his com-set, Malone informed the rest of his team that the hostages had been recovered, and they were ready to haul ass to the extraction point. "Pick up the action, boys, so we can slip out of here and get a head start.

The sound of gunfire immediately increased from the blackness surrounding the camp. Anderson, Nichols, and then KC carrying Fisher, filed out of the hut, disappearing over a nearby hill as fast as possible in absolute silence. KC had no trouble carrying the unconscious man on his back over the treacherous terrain. The lieutenant barely weighed a hundred and forty pounds after his ordeal. The four men were met by two other camouflaged SEALs about fifty yards out. One took point, leading the group, while the other man and Anderson covered the rear to ensure they weren't followed. Even though it was still dark, the humidity hung on the men like wet blankets, and while the SEAL team was used to conditions as miserable as this, the hostages were weak from abuse and malnutrition. Anderson had to grab Nichols several times when the captain stumbled.

Three minutes after they cleared the first hill, KC's team gave the all-clear, and he passed it on to the Army support staff back at base. In his head, he counted off thirty seconds, and then the remaining tangos and village exploded under a U.S. airstrike. At the same time, the last of the team caught up with the others. A few moments later, the helicopter which would carry them away from this hellhole appeared and landed half a football field away. Ducking low as they approached, the team climbed on board with the two rescued soldiers, and then the big military bird lifted back off the ground. The well-practiced landing and takeoff had taken less than ninety seconds.

KC glanced around and surveyed his team—all were present and accounted for, with no signs of injuries. The hostages were alive and secure. Lieutenant Fisher was already being tended to by the team medic and showed signs of awakening. *Thank God*. It had been another successful mission. He wished they all went this smoothly, but that was like praying for the sky to fall. There were no guarantees in his business. The older he got, the more that sad fact was proven.

He felt Captain Nichols, who was seated next to him, tap him on his upper arm. "Not that I'm ungrateful for you rescuing us, but Army is still going to kick Navy's fucking ass at the next football game."

"I don't think so, sir. *Hoo-yah*!"

The helicopter cabin erupted in a chorus of *hoo-yahs*, followed by relieved laughter as everyone relaxed and settled in for the long ride back to the base. KC closed his eyes and looked forward to heading home for four weeks of well-deserved leave.

"What do you fucking mean you can't find her? It's a two-bit, fucking town without a fucking Walmart. How big can the place fucking be?"

Leo Simmons cringed at the chewing out he was getting over the cell phone. He'd fucked up big time, and Hernandez was giving him a chance to fix it. If he didn't find the bitch and the money, he was as good as dead when the drug dealer got his hands on him. Running would be futile since the man had connections across the U.S. Maybe he could make it over the Canadian border or down into Mexico before they caught up to him. But he'd rather find Susan's sister and put a bullet in her brain for taking what was his . . . well, not really his, but his boss's.

When Hernandez stopped his rant to take a breath, Simmons tried to placate him. "The guy at the motel said she'd already left. We checked the bus depot and then drove up and down the main strip. There's no sign of her, but we'll keep looking."

"You fucking better. This is your fucking screw-up. Fix it!"

The call disconnected, and he wanted to throw the phone at the brick wall of the convenience store they were parked next to. That bitch had to be here somewhere. A cop ran her license late last night somewhere in this hick town. Apparently, she got into a car accident with a bunch of chicks. Simmons and two of Hernandez's flunkies had driven all night to get here, but the fucking cunt was nowhere to be found. They couldn't even find the car the chicks were in to ask them about her.

Kicking a bottle across the parking lot in frustration, he strode back to the Cadillac where his partners for this trip were waiting. Climbing in the back seat, he slammed the door. "Let's drive around again. That bitch has to be here somewhere."

Chapter 2

Releasing a heavy sigh, KC turned off his car's engine in the driveway of his uncle's beach house. The small, blue cottage was trimmed in white and sported a quaint widow's walk while resting just beyond the dunes of the pristine shoreline. Facing the Atlantic Ocean on the Outer Banks, the three-bedroom house sat on the edge of a sleepy little town named Whisper, North Carolina. The town was more of a small, tight community, where everyone knew everyone else, instead of a bustling tourist area. Not that it mattered to KC one way or the other. He just needed a place to crash when he was on leave from "saving the world," as his Uncle Dan proudly told everyone.

Whisper, being about ninety minutes south of where his SEAL team was stationed in Little Creek, Virginia, was the perfect place to wind down and recharge his body and mind. KC was so exhausted he didn't know if he had the strength to get from his vehicle to the back door and then into his bedroom before he fell fast asleep. Taking a deep, cleansing breath, he forced himself to open the car door, grab his canvas duffel, and shuffle his way to the porch. He loved the smell of the salt water—fresh and crisp. It was part of the reason he'd joined the Navy instead of one of the other branches of the military.

The other reason was the impression a retired Navy SEAL had made during KC's high school's career day many years ago. He saw the proud, steel look in the man's eyes as he described the intense training and commitment required of all SEALs, and KC knew right then he wanted to experience it for himself. With his uncle's encouragement, he'd enlisted as soon as he graduated from high school, and five years later he'd survived the grueling six-month SEAL BUD/s (Basic Underwater Demolition/SEAL) training program. He had proudly served in the Navy ever since.

Putting his key into the lock of the back door, he felt the weeks of cumulating tension begin to purge from his body. This place was his comfort zone—his Eden. The cottage and its surrounding area always fortified him, and it wouldn't take long for him to feel like a normal person again. It would temporarily rid him of the feeling of walking a very long tightrope, worrying if the current mission would be the one when he or one of his teammates didn't come home alive.

KC couldn't pinpoint when the job had gone from an adrenaline rush to an extremely stressful career, but at thirty-five, he wondered if maybe his time in the SEALs was over. For the fourth time since he'd left the base, he contemplated taking the position of SEAL Training Instructor, which had been offered to him. He'd turned it down twice in the past because he was dedicated to his team and didn't want to leave them, but now he was having second thoughts. Not about his team because, aside from his uncle and two brothers, the men in SEAL Team Six were family to him. However, the missions they'd been on lately were starting to take a toll on him—mentally, as well as physically. As things stood now, he was still up in the air about his decision, but he'd have plenty of time to think about it during his month-long leave. For now, though, he only wanted to climb into bed. In his current condition and mindset, he felt like he could sleep for at least forty-eight hours straight before his body finally rejuvenated itself.

Letting his military green duffel drop inside the door with a thud, KC relocked the deadbolt, flipped the light switch on, turned around, and froze.

Fuck a damn duck.

The last thing he expected when he arrived at his uncle's place was to be confronted by a slim, auburn-haired woman. She was wearing nothing but a terrified look on her face and a thin white T-shirt, which barely reached her shapely thighs. She was also pointing a black and very deadly, semi-automatic 9mm at his chest.

"Who the hell are you, and how'd you get in here?" the woman demanded. The strength of her voice was in total contrast to the fear in her eyes and the unsteadiness with which she held the heavy gun in her outstretched hands.

What the fuck had he just walked in on? Some transient who broke in, looking for a place to sleep? Well, if she was a transient, she was a darn cute one. Damn, he really was tired if he thought an intruder with a gun was cute.

He held his arms out, palms open, to show her he wasn't armed—well, he was, he just wasn't prepared to let this crazed woman know it yet. KC kept his voice low and calm. "I could be asking you the same thing."

"I asked you first." Her weapon remained pointed at him as she inched her way to the left, putting several pieces of furniture between them.

He kept his demeanor and hands steady. "This is my

uncle's place, and I stay here when I'm in town. Now, why don't you lower that gun before someone gets hurt?"

The woman narrowed her shockingly-blue eyes. Even at the distance separating them, he could see they were the color of the shallow waters of the Caribbean Sea. Nevertheless, she showed no signs of relinquishing her perceived vantage point. "That someone is going to be you if you move a muscle. I rented this cottage from Dan Malone, and he didn't mention anything about a nephew."

"That's impossible." KC shook his head slowly in disbelief. "Uncle Dan would never rent this place."

Her chin tilted up in defiance despite the slight tremor in it. "Well, apparently, he would, and he did. Three days ago. To me. Now leave."

KC noticed the gun's weight was taking its toll on the woman's extended arms as they began to shake and sway. He let out a loud, weary sigh. "What can I say or do to convince you to set the gun down, or better yet, put it away?"

"You can leave, that's what you can do."

"Sorry, honey, that's not going to happen." He noticed her eyes flared in silent fury at the personal endearment. "What else?"

"If you're Dan Malone's nephew, prove it." Her tone told him no matter what he said, it wouldn't make a difference to her.

KC scanned the room and realized if his uncle did lease the cottage to this insane woman, he'd kept it fully furnished. Nothing had changed, and all his uncle's things still decorated the comfortable room. There was no evidence of personal items which might belong to the woman who stood before him. Even though he thought it was strange, he ignored the simple fact for the moment and pointed to the mantle over the red brick fireplace. "The picture on the left is of my uncle, brothers, and me on a fishing trip last year. My hair's a little longer now, but that's me on the far right. I'm in most of the photos around the room, but that's the most recent."

He stayed perfectly still as the woman made her way over to the fireplace to look at the picture, keeping enough distance between her and KC to ensure he wouldn't attack her. He knew he could easily overtake her, but she was obviously scared, and there was no point in anyone being hurt unnecessarily. She glanced quickly at the photo and then back at him but didn't say a word. Evidently, she was still wary.

"And the football trophy next to it is from my senior year of high school when we won the state championship. It has my name on it. If you let me take my wallet out, I can show you my license."

The woman thought about it for a moment, then nodded. "OK, but slowly."

KC eased his leather wallet out of his back pocket and tossed it on the floor at her feet. Keeping the gun trained on him, she cautiously lowered herself to the ground to pick it up. Opening the smooth leather case, she studied his license and then tossed the brown wallet back to him. He caught it in his right hand and slowly returned it to his rear pocket, keeping his left hand where she could see it.

The tension in her face and shoulders eased a little, but she still kept the weapon pointed at him. "Okay, I'm convinced you *are* related to Mr. Malone, but it doesn't explain what you're doing sneaking in here in the middle of the night, scaring the hell out of me. You have to leave. Now!"

KC let out another frustrated sigh. The situation was getting old and annoying really fast. "Look. I already proved

I'm Dan's nephew. Can you put away the damn gun before you accidentally shoot me?"

Her hand shook. "How do you know it would be an accident and not on purpose?"

Oh, for fuck's sake. He lowered his arms and bent to retrieve his duffel bag, only a smidgen faster than a snail's pace so as not to alarm her. "Look, lady, I wasn't sneaking in here. I still don't know who you are, and right now, I'm too fucking exhausted to give a damn. Shoot me, or let me go to bed. It's two o'clock in the morning, and I haven't had more than a two-hour nap in over fifty-four hours."

Her jaw dropped as he began to walk toward the hallway which led to the two downstairs bedrooms. "But . . . but you can't stay here."

He stopped and glared at her over his shoulder. "Why the hell not? It's the middle of the night, and I'm about to drop dead of exhaustion. I'm not getting back into my car to find another place to sleep when there's a comfortable bed just down the hall. I'm also not going to hurt you. Trust me, you're safer with me than almost anyone else. We'll work this out in the morning. Right now, I'm going to go to sleep."

The woman stared at him in shock, mouth agape, gun in hand, as he strode down the hall. He entered the smaller of the two bedrooms, shut the door behind him with a faint resounding click, and turned the lock. He honestly didn't think she would shoot him, but it was better to be safe than sorry.

What the fuck was Uncle Dan up to now? She had to be someone the older man decided to help—he was always coming to the aid of people down on their luck. And from the look of her, she fit the Dan Malone profile of a person who could use a helping hand. While he wouldn't deny she had been sexy as sin in her T-shirt, pretending to be a female Rambo, she was a little too skinny. And the dark circles under her eyes appeared to be from more than having her beauty sleep interrupted. It was too late to wake his uncle up, although KC was tempted, so he quickly stripped down to his boxer briefs and literally fell into bed. The last image in his mind as sleep overtook him was a pair of long legs and a white T-shirt.

Chapter 3

hat the hell? Moriah lowered herself to the couch and continued to stare at the door the stranger had closed moments before. She still wasn't sure what had just happened or why the man, KC he'd called himself, was still here and what she would do about it. There was no way she could go back to sleep with a strange man across the hallway from her room. She couldn't force him to leave on her own, he'd proven that. She also didn't want to call Mr. Malone in the middle of the night to come over and get his nephew out of there. And she definitely didn't want to call the police to remove him—that would result in too many questions she couldn't answer. Moriah reluctantly realized her only option was to make a pot of coffee, stay up, and wait until KC woke up. Then she would convince him he had to leave. If he wouldn't, she'd have to hit the road and disappear again.

Four miserable hours later, Moriah was still sitting on the couch, the gun on the cushion beside her within easy reach, as she sipped her third cup of coffee. She didn't know why she bothered drinking the potent brew because it made her more nervous than she already was. Glancing around, she surveyed the family photos scattered about the room. Many of them were of Dan Malone, KC, and his brothers, who were all quite handsome. Some photos were obviously of the boys in their youth with their uncle, and others were with a couple who she assumed were their parents. In one picture, the three pre-pubescent boys were dressed as cowboys. In another photo, they were wearing pint-sized military uniforms.

There were also pictures of a much younger Dan and a beautiful blonde woman, and from how they looked at each other, it was apparent they were very much in love. Moriah wondered who the woman was and where she was today. Scanning the multiple frames around the room and in the hallway, she couldn't find any pictures of the woman in recent years or updated photos of the boys' parents.

The Malone's appeared to be a close-knit family, and Moriah sighed, wishing hers had been the same while she was growing up in Chicago. Her so-called father finally left her mother for good when Moriah was a teenager, after several long absences over the years. By that time, the dream of an ideal childhood had long since faded away. She knew her mother wanted, and tried, to be there for her and her sister, but she worked long hours at two jobs to ensure a roof over their heads and food on the table. Her work and sleep occupied most, if not all, of her time.

Fourteen-year-old Moriah had taught herself to cook and helped around the house with laundry and cleaning. She'd tried to give her younger sister a sense of consistency and lead her in the right direction. Still, Susan, then eleven, was more interested in boys and eventually drugs than listening to her sibling. While Moriah was in their apartment doing her chores and homework, Susan was running with the wrong crowd and finding endless trouble to get caught up in.

There were times she barely avoided being sent to juvenile detention. Now, Moriah wondered if her sister had ended up there, would she have turned her life around and still be alive today, or would the results have been the same?

Susan's wild and promiscuous lifestyle caught up to her when she became pregnant at seventeen. The child's father denied the baby was his and left town before he was born. But little Nicholas became a stabilizing rod for Susan as she tried to mature and become a good mother to her child. She agreed to drug counseling and found an evening job as a waitress at a local restaurant. With the extra income, their mother was able to quit her second job and help care for the baby.

The little boy became the light of Moriah's life. She loved to come home from her part-time job or classes at the local community college to play with him. The sisters and their mother doted on him as much as possible, and Nicholas was a happy child, if not a little spoiled. Moriah loved going to the local dollar store, since that was all she could afford, and finding a new toy for him or borrowing children's books from the library. Whenever she could, she'd read to him aloud, and it quickly became their favorite time together. As soon as Moriah finished one book, he'd hand her another one. She lost count of how many times she'd read *Winnie the Pooh* to him.

Things went very smoothly for the family for a few years. Nicholas had grown into a bubbly five-year-old and peppered everyone with "why" questions from morning until night. His grandmother appeared younger and more relaxed than she had in years. Susan was staying clean, and Moriah was one semester away from her teaching degree. It seemed as if things were finally going well for all of them.

But about seven months ago, Moriah started to notice the tell-tale signs that Susan was using drugs again. Her sister would suddenly be short of money and had to borrow from Moriah and her mother. She'd begun asking them to babysit Nicholas more and more. She would also come home much later from the end of her shift at the local Chili's, and Moriah was left wondering if her sister still had the job. The most noticeable change was Susan's appearance, which began to go downhill as she cared less and less about her clothes and hygiene. Her weight dropped drastically. Moriah knew all the signs pointed to a crack cocaine user—hell, their seedy neighborhood was full of them.

Through the neighborhood grapevine, she'd discovered her sister was dating a small-time drug dealer named Leo Simmons. Moriah knew the asshole by reputation only. He'd started pushing drugs on his high school classmates before he was arrested and expelled for possession. At the time, he was still a minor, so the courts gave him a slap on the wrist and a short stint in juvenile detention. After his release, he returned to the drug business, and if the rumors she'd heard were true, he was being protected by a few crooked cops.

Moriah had given her sister an ultimatum, break up with the dirtbag or move out—without Nicholas. Moriah refused to allow her nephew to be exposed to his mother's dangerous lifestyle. Susan begged forgiveness and swore she would stop seeing Leo. She cleaned herself up again and, for a few short weeks, appeared to be back on the right track. Moriah would never stop blaming herself for taking Susan's word that everything would be okay.

Shifting on the couch for what seemed like the hundredth time in the past hour, she stared out the row of windows facing the beach. The sun was beginning its slow crawl up the clear horizon, bathing the sky in hues of ripe pineapples, cherries, and tangerines. It was so beautiful and peaceful at the shore, and Moriah wished she could live here forever. The sounds of the pounding surf had comforted her over the past few days. She'd loved the feel of the silky sand between her toes during the few times she'd dared to venture out onto the beach.

Charming was how she would describe Whisper, North Carolina. She'd seen the center of the little town twice. Once, when Dan Malone had driven her through it on the way to the cottage, and then again, when she'd taken a cab to the grocery store to stock up on a week's worth of food. It was the type of town where people could easily walk around the mile length of stores and municipal buildings instead of driving. She wondered if they held picnics and parades in the main square on the 4th of July or any other day. She'd read about many small towns which celebrated that way in the romance books she'd cherished since she was a teenager. A voracious reader, she couldn't get enough of books. Since arriving in Whisper five days ago, she had already gone through two local history books she'd found on a shelf in the cottage and was currently on chapter five of a well-read copy of *Jaws*.

Growing up in Chicago, Moriah could never imagine living in a place that didn't bustle twenty-four hours a day, seven days a week. She was, however, beginning to think she could learn to enjoy the slow pace and quiet atmosphere of a small community. It was too bad she wouldn't be around long enough to find out.

As the sun continued its climb in the east, the rest of the morning sky turned into a colorful mural, and Moriah contemplated her unexpected visitor. KC was incredibly good-looking, and she was annoyed at herself for noticing. Well, any woman with a pulse would have noticed, she told herself.

With broad shoulders and a chiseled chest and back, he stood about six-five, which was taller than most of the men she knew. Thick medium-brown hair hung a few inches past the nape of his neck, and his wicked, hazel eyes were captivating. A scar over his right temple almost ruined what could be a movie-star face. He hadn't used a razor in several days, which added to his bad-boy attractiveness. In a snug black T-shirt and tan cargo pants, it had been blatantly obvious he was in excellent physical shape, and she wondered how he managed to stay that way.

Shaking her head, Moriah tried to rid her mind of the images of the man. In a few hours, she would convince him to leave, then try to figure out what she would do next. Dan Malone hadn't run a credit check on her when she rented the cottage from him, nor did he ask her to sign a lease. She didn't tell him she wouldn't be staying long and let him assume she would be around for a while. No one in Whisper had any idea who she really was. And no one knew the horror which had taken over her world four short months ago and left her running for her life.

Shit, she missed her family. *Don't think about them. Don't think about Momma, Susan, and Nicholas. There's nothing you can do for them now. You're safe for a few days. Just think about what you're going to do next and where you'll go from here.*

Moriah glanced at the closed bedroom door and prayed she was safe for now.

Dan Malone straightened up his small kitchen as he waited for the pot of coffee to brew. His rescued Labrador mix, Jinx, lay across the threshold between the kitchen and living area, waiting patiently. A combination of at least three breeds, the gentle but protective mutt was the perfect companion for a single, older man. Approximately six years old, he was completely charcoal black except for the very tip of his tail and the area around his muzzle, which were stark white. As a result of his coloring, the big dog appeared to have a permanent grin. As a puppy, before he'd found his forever home, his tail had somehow been broken, and it hung at a crooked angle. He was very affectionate, and Dan adored his canine sidekick. The dog never argued with or heckled him like his three nephews enjoyed doing. Jinx was definitely his best friend in life, and neither of them would have it any other way.

After the last of his nephews had ventured off into the military, Dan had found the beach house too quiet and moved into the one-bedroom apartment above the hardware store he owned. He preferred to keep both places exceptionally tidy. There was never any clutter, and everything was kept in its proper place—a throwback to his Army days, he supposed.

Filling a large thermos with his daily dose of caffeine, which he would take downstairs to the shop, he wondered if KC had arrived at the cottage and met Maura yet. He chuckled to himself, wishing he could be a fly on the wall for that encounter. Well, he was sure he'd hear about it soon enough.

He was a true romantic at heart and thought it was about time his three nephews, KC, Brian, and Sean, became ones, too—with a little help on his part, of course. Dan had lost his one and only true love at twenty-nine after barely two years of marriage. Falling hopelessly in love on a blind date, he and Annie had eloped after knowing each other for three weeks. When she was diagnosed with leukemia almost a year later, at the tender age of twenty-four, she'd begged him to leave her.

"This isn't what you expected or deserved when you married me," she'd told him.

But Dan had refused to abandon her. They'd spent as much time together as possible, and between his job and her treatments and doctor visits, they'd lived and loved life to the fullest. They'd gone for long walks on the beach and picnics in the park. He would take her to interesting places he'd heard of or drive them around aimlessly just to see different landscapes.

She'd never been on a plane, and one day, he'd arranged for an army pilot buddy of his to take them up in his private four-passenger aircraft. She'd been able to experience the thrill of flying above the earth and loved every minute of it. And he'd loved the smile that had remained on her face for hours after they'd returned home.

Most of the time, though, they'd sat on the porch of the beach house they called home, watching the sunrises and listening to the pounding surf. He'd cherished every moment with her, greedily storing memories for the future. And at the end, he'd held his sweet Annie close to his chest as she passed into the afterlife and vowed he would love her always.

In the years following his wife's death, Dan Malone became known throughout the small community as a collector of strays—animal and human. He was always bringing home lost or injured animals, much to Jinx's dismay, despite the dog being a rescued stray himself. Dan would heal those he could before finding homes for each one of the wayward domesticated animals. The wild ones, he would release back into their habitats once they were able to survive on their own.

When it came to people, he never met someone in need who he didn't try to assist, even if it was only in some small way. Sometimes it was buying a meal or giving someone a ride. Other times it might involve offering a few dollars to help the individual get by. Maura Jennings was his new pet project, and in her case, she needed a place to stay.

Dan knew there was more to Maura's story than what she'd let on. He had a sixth sense when it came to people like her. She'd told him she was recovering from an abusive relationship and was looking for a new place to start over. He suspected, however, there was a lot more she wasn't telling him. She appeared to be a strong woman, physically and mentally, and Dan couldn't believe she would ever allow a man to strike her or abuse her in any manner, at least not after the first time. Yet, he was a good judge of character and knew whatever she was running from, the young woman needed his help.

For now, he was letting her stay at the cottage and hoped KC would be able to get her to open up to him. It would probably be therapeutic for both of them. She needed a protector, and KC needed to focus on something other than his career for a change. Dan knew his nephew was considering leaving his SEAL team for a stateside position. Maybe if he had someone waiting for him at home every night, the decision would be easier to make.

Chapter 4

It wasn't until one o'clock in the afternoon that Moriah became aware of KC moving around in his bedroom. She heard the toilet flushing and then the shower running, and she began to pace the kitchen floor. Since she'd waited this long to talk to him, she guessed she could wait a little longer. Once he finished washing up, she would advise him he had to leave and find another place to stay. As she straightened up the already tidy kitchen, she tried to think of how she could kick him out without sounding as rude as she'd been earlier. Undoubtedly, he wasn't a man who would willingly take orders from her, so she would have to try and charm him.

After she'd recovered from his appearance and subsequent disappearance, during the middle of the night, she'd gone back to the bedroom she was using and threw on a pair of sweatpants with a matching zip-up jacket. Then about an hour ago, she'd jumped in the shower and re-dressed into a large red T-shirt, which covered the gun she'd tucked into the back of the waistband of her jeans, and a pair of sneakers. Her long hair was up in a loose ponytail, and her face was devoid of makeup. She'd almost put on her usual eyeliner and blush but then reminded herself she wasn't trying to attract KC. In fact, she wanted to do the opposite. She wanted him out of there as soon as possible so that she could get some much-needed sleep. And then, she would be able to plan her next move.

Moriah jumped a little as KC's bedroom door swung open without warning. While daydreaming, she hadn't realized the shower had stopped. Turning her back to the counter, she waited as he came down the hallway and entered the tiny kitchen off the main living room. If she had thought the room wasn't that big before, it got even smaller as the mountainous man filled it. His wet hair was gleaming from the shower, and his face was now cleanly shaven. She'd thought he would look less intimidating without the scruff but realized that wasn't the case. Just the man's presence was nerve-racking as her body had an unwanted response to him. Moisture pooled between her legs, and her nipples hardened, forcing her to cross her arms over them. He'd donned another snug T-shirt, this one was gray, and replaced his cargo pants with a pair of faded jeans, which were molded to his body in all the right places. He was barefoot, and for a split second, Moriah wondered why she'd never noticed before that a man's feet could be sexy. She tore her eyes away from him, horrified at the direction her thoughts had taken.

KC barely glanced at her as he went straight to the cabinet above the coffee maker and grabbed a large mug. Her eyes flicked back to him and roamed over his broad shoulders and strong back. She tried her damnedest to keep her gaze above his waist but wasn't successful.

Damn, he has a beautiful ass.

He poured himself some coffee before returning the glass pot to its holder, then pivoted to lean his hips against the counter and crossed his ankles. And since she had been staring at his ass, she was now staring at his groin and the large bulge behind the denim. Blushing, she turned away and tried to busy herself by wiping down the spotless table for two.

Taking a large gulp of the brew, he grimaced and said his first words of the day to her. "How the hell do you drink this stuff? It's awful."

Keeping her eyes averted, Moriah shrugged as she brushed invisible crumbs into her waiting hand. "Well, it's been sitting there since 2:00 a.m."

KC dumped the coffee from both the mug and carafe down the sink and set about making a new pot. As it brewed, he rifled through the refrigerator and pantry, taking out what he needed, apparently making himself bacon, eggs, and toast. Moriah didn't think this was the time to point out that he was eating her groceries. If he was aware of her eyes following him around the room, he didn't acknowledge it. Finding a skillet and utensils with ease was further proof he was comfortable and familiar with the cottage. She wondered if she should wait until he'd finished preparing his meal to ask him to leave or if she should take the plunge and start talking.

With his back to her as he placed several slices of bacon into a skillet on the stove, KC put her dilemma on hold. "Are you hungry?"

She cleared her throat. "Uh, no, thanks. I ate earlier."

He grunted in response and kept his eyes on his cooking. "So, do you have a name?"

Moriah hesitated a moment before making sure she gave him the fake name she had used for the past few weeks. She would change it again after she left Whisper anyway, and his uncle already knew her by the alias. "Maura Jennings."

Removing the bacon and adding four eggs to the skillet, he then popped two pieces of bread into the nearby toaster.

"Well, Maura Jennings, why don't you tell me about yourself, hmm?"

She stared at him, wary of his questions. "Like what?"

"Oh, I don't know . . . like . . . how come you're renting my uncle's place and why you threatened to shoot me with a 9mm last night?"

He still didn't turn around, and Moriah stared at his muscular back while trying to think of an answer he would accept. "A single woman can never be too careful. The gun is for protection. You never know when some lunatic will break in at two o'clock in the morning."

KC clearly heard the sarcasm she'd added with that last sentence. He gave her a quick glance over his shoulder and then went back to making his breakfast. "I said it last night, and I'll say it again. I *didn't* break in. I have a key. And last time I had a psych exam, they determined I wasn't a lunatic . . . or so they told me."

What? Was he fucking kidding her? Why the hell was he having psych exams? Maybe she *should* have called the police.

He put the sunny-side-up eggs next to the bacon on a plate, added the buttered toast, then carried his meal to the small bistro set in the corner of the room. As he sat, his gaze flashed toward her, and a smirk spread across his face when he saw her eyes and mouth were wide open while she stared at him. "That was a joke, Maura. I'm in the military. My job requires me to go through a psych exam every once in a while."

Relief washed over her. Closing her mouth, she felt her shoulders relax a tad. "Oh. Okay."

She leaned against the counter by the sink and studied him as he ate. His jaw tightened and relaxed as he chewed. Muscular arms rippled as he moved the fork from the plate to his mouth and back again.

And, oh, what a mouth it was. His lips were both hard and

soft looking, and Moriah wondered what it would be like to be kissed by lips like his. She bet he was a talented kisser. The man was fucking gorgeous, and there was no way he hadn't worked his way through hundreds of women over the years. She was curious what his face would look like if those exquisite lips ever turned up into a real smile.

Suddenly conscious of ogling him, Moriah cleared her throat again. "So, is your name C-a-s-e-y or K-C?"

"It's K-C, as in Kevin Christopher." At her raised eyebrow, he added, "Nobody's called me by my full name since I was a kid, and then, only when I was in trouble."

She tilted her head in curiosity. "Were you in trouble a lot as a kid?"

"That's putting it mildly." He pointed his fork at her. "But we're not talking about me, we're talking about you."

Moriah gave him what she hoped appeared to be a bored shrug of her shoulders. "What's to talk about? I needed a place to stay, and your uncle was kind enough to rent me his house."

After finishing the bacon and eggs, he soaked up the remaining yolks with his toast. "Where're you from?"

"Los Angeles," she lied. Why was he so damn inquisitive?

Swallowing the last of his breakfast, KC raised an eyebrow at her. "That's odd. You don't have a west-coast accent. More like from the middle states."

Dropping her gaze to the floor to hide her astonishment at being caught in a fib, Moriah shrugged again. "Well, my family moved around a lot. I didn't even know I had an accent."

He stared at her for a few moments, and she fought the urge to squirm under the scrutiny. If he suspected she was lying further, he let it go for now. "So, how did you end up in our little town of Whisper, and where did you meet my uncle?"

At least this part of what she was willing to tell him was true. "I've been traveling around a lot and ended up at the Walmart over in Elizabeth City. Your uncle noticed me looking at apartment rentals posted on the bulletin board and offered to rent me this place."

Dan Malone had approached her to see if she needed any assistance. He said she seemed "lost." Not trusting a male stranger, Moriah started to walk away from him but stopped when he mentioned a house available for cheap rent. Still skeptical, she took his proffered driver's license and cell phone. He instructed her to call information for the Dare County Sheriff's Department phone number and then ask for the sheriff or one of his office staff to verify his identity. Mary Schreiber, the secretary, had confirmed Dan Malone was a good friend of the sheriff's, an upstanding citizen, and he did, indeed, own an empty beach house. She'd also said Dan was a kind man who was always helping those in need and could be thoroughly trusted.

With the glowing endorsement and no better options, despite the man being friends with the local sheriff, Moriah took him up on his offer to rent his cottage. He even allowed her to hold his cell phone when he realized she didn't have one until they arrived at the beach house just so she would feel safer. Moriah knew she was crazy to trust someone she didn't know, but there was something in Dan Malone's soft, brown eyes that convinced her he was one of the good guys in life. And Lord knew she hadn't met many of them.

"Yeah, that sounds like Uncle Dan. He's always bringing in strays." At her insulted expression, he added, "No offense."

"None taken," she mumbled. She didn't mention the comment struck a chord in her. A "stray" was kind of close to how she felt—all alone in the world, moving from place to place, just trying to survive.

Picking up his plate, KC rinsed it off and placed it into the dishwasher along with the fork and knife. He cleaned, dried, and put away the skillet and spatula he'd used, and then wiped down the cooking area with expertise.

As he finished his chores, she put an expectant look on her face. "So, you'll be leaving now?"

He spun around slowly, crossed his muscular arms over his equally powerful chest, and leaned his hips against the counter. "What makes you think that?"

"Well, um . . ." she stuttered as she mirrored the position of his arms and cocked her hip. *Be firm.* "You can't stay here. I paid Mr. Malone my rent, and I don't want or need a housemate."

His narrowed eyes seemed to smolder as they briefly dropped to her ample chest, which had been thrust upward with her annoyed stance. "What do you want then?"

Moriah's mouth dropped open again, stunned at the suggestiveness in his tone, but after several moments of silence, he shook his head as if clearing his mind. He straightened and brought his gaze back to her face. "I'll tell you what. I'll talk to Uncle Dan and ask if I can crash on his couch. It shouldn't be any problem, although it's not as comfortable as my bed here."

She nodded but continued to gape at him as he exited the kitchen. A few moments later, with his sneakers on and keys in hand, KC left without saying another word. It would be another ten minutes before Moriah realized he'd left the rest of his things in the smaller bedroom. She wasn't sure if she was upset or pleased to know he would have to return for them. And the indecision worried her.

Chapter 5

"So, as usual, you know nothing about Ms. Maura Jennings. She's just another needy person in a long line of needy people."

KC helped restock the shelves in the hardware store while he chastised his uncle. The closest nationwide home-improvement store was about fifteen miles away, so most of the locals still used Malone's Hardware for convenience and out of a sense of loyalty. In addition to everything a good hardware store kept in stock, Dan also kept a moderate supply of fishing gear and frozen bait for the anglers in the community. Behind the counter were many pictures of very impressive catches made by some of the locals over the years, including a few from KC and his brothers.

The older man sliced open another box of latex paint with the box-cutter he was never without. "I know she's in some sort of trouble and needs help. What else is there to know?"

KC raised an eyebrow at Dan but continued to work. "Did you ever stop to think that maybe she *was* trouble and not *in* trouble?"

"Nope, and neither did you."

Despite rolling his eyes, he knew his uncle was right. He'd seen genuine fear in Maura's eyes last night and wondered, if she had to, could she actually have fired the gun at him?

Handing him two more gallons of semi-gloss paint, Dan continued. "She told me she'd been in an abusive relationship and finally got the courage to leave the guy. She has no family and decided to travel a bit before figuring out where she wants to settle down. She's afraid the ex-boyfriend will come after her."

"That would explain the gun."

Dan froze in surprise. "Gun? What gun?"

He reached over and grabbed the paint cans his uncle held suspended in mid-air. "The one she pulled on me when I let myself into the cottage at two in the morning."

Dan chuckled. "Got the jump on you, *eh*? I would've given good money to see that."

"You could have warned me, you know."

"But where would the fun be in that?" Dan laughed louder as he slapped his oldest nephew on the back. The two of them gathered the empty boxes and tossed them into the rear stock room before heading back to the front of the store. Jimmy, the teenager who worked at the store after school, would break the boxes down later for recycling.

KC followed his uncle to the counter and crouched down to rub Jinx's belly. Snoring on his back in a sunbeam by the front door, the large dog slept with all four paws in the air. As he straightened again, KC muttered, "Useless mutt."

His uncle began to restock a rack of batteries behind the counter. "Jinx would resent that if he was awake."

"When I see him earn his keep, maybe I'll change my opinion of him. Until then, he's nothing but a useless mutt."

Dan looked over his shoulder and eyed his nephew curiously. "So, what did you think?"

Unsure what the man was talking about, KC tilted his head. "About what?"

"Not what, *who*. Maura. She's a looker, don't you think?"

Glancing around the store, he avoided making eye contact with his uncle. "I really hadn't noticed."

The bald-faced lie received a loud snort. "Sure you didn't."

KC knew better than to deny it further—of course, he'd fucking noticed. After all, he was a healthy, heterosexual male, and Maura wasn't just a looker, she was downright fucking gorgeous. In the middle of the night, after he closed his bedroom door, he'd been hard as granite, and it wasn't from the adrenaline of having a gun pointed at him. It'd been a response to all her exposed, feminine flesh. Ever since he'd eyed those long, sexy legs extending downward from the skimpy T-shirt she'd apparently worn to bed, he could think of nothing else. Well, except maybe what the T-shirt hadn't shown. It had hung on her slim figure, molding itself to her curves in all the right places. The darkness of her nipples had been visible through the thin cotton. He could imagine the weight of her breasts in his hands as his thumbs brushed over their stiff peaks.

She had beautiful, auburn hair, which fell to the middle of her back. He'd been disappointed to see it pulled up into a ponytail when he found her in the kitchen earlier. His hand had itched for him to walk over and release the silky strands from their bondage. The reddish-brown color was a perfect contrast to her pale, porcelain skin and sexy, baby-blue eyes. She was an erotic beauty from head to toe. As his younger brother Sean would say, she was a walking hard-on. Yup, he had definitely noticed.

Shaking the vision from his mind before his body could react to it again, he changed the subject. "I was a little surprised you rented the house. None of us have stayed there for more than a week or two in years. Hell, since you live above this place, I'm amazed you never sold it. It's got to be worth a small fortune in today's market."

"Renting it to someone in need is one thing, but you know I would never sell it." His uncle sounded wistful. "Annie and I bought the place a few weeks after we were married. Scraped together every penny we could and mortgaged it to the hilt. Even when money was tight, your aunt decorated the place really nice. She and I painted every room ourselves after she spent hours picking out just the right colors. Annie would scour yard sales and make something useful and beautiful from other people's junk. Even on her sickest days, she would be telling me to move something, or dust something, or fluff something, just to be sure everything was perfect."

KC smiled. He'd heard this story many times since he was a kid, and as it always did, it made him wish he'd known his aunt. She had passed away long before the Malone brothers were born, but they were raised with stories of Aunt Annie. He knew a small bit of his Uncle Dan had died along with his wife many years ago.

"Even though we only had two wonderful years together there, it will always be our place. I could never give it up. And someday it will belong to you and your brothers . . ." He pointed to KC with a frown. "And if you ever sell it, I'll come back from the grave and haunt your sorry asses!"

KC's smile got even bigger. "I'm sure you will. But now that you've rented it temporarily, I need a place to crash, so I guess it'll be on your couch."

"Um, that's impossible."

"Why?" he asked as his eyes narrowed. When his uncle avoided looking him straight in the face, his suspicions grew.

"Well, you see . . . Jinx kind of ate something which didn't agree with him last week and got sick all over the couch. It stunk to high heaven, and I couldn't get the stains out, so I had to get rid of it. I haven't had time to go pick out a new one yet."

The younger man frowned, and he glared at the sleeping dog. "I told you he was a useless mutt. Now, I have to find another place to crash for four weeks or until you replace your damn couch. Guess I'll call Brian."

"Uh, that won't work either."

Sigh. "Why the hell not?"

"One of his buddies from the police department was kicked out by his wife, so the guy has been bunking on Brian's couch until he finds an apartment."

"Great, just great. What the fuck am I supposed to do now?" KC put his hands on his hips in exasperation. He didn't want to drive back to Little Creek and spend his leave on the base, and Sean lived too far away in Florida. He still had many friends in Whisper, but none he wanted to impose on for a month.

"Watch your language, and there's a perfectly good bed back at the cottage."

Dan pretended to readjust a few things on the shelf behind the counter to hide his smile, but KC still noticed it anyway. *What the fuck is the old man up to?* "Your renter has made it perfectly clear she doesn't want a housemate."

"She has, has she? Well then, why don't I just talk to Maura, explain the problem, and see if she wouldn't mind putting up with your surly butt for a few days?" He shrugged. "Until I get a new couch, that is."

KC grunted. "I'm not surly." He ignored his uncle's snort of disagreement. "And I don't need you to solve my problems for me. I'll talk to her."

A chuckle escaped his uncle. "Well, the least you could do is turn on some of the famous Malone charm you allegedly inherited instead of looking like an ogre."

He laughed even harder when KC rolled his eyes and pasted an unnatural smile on his face before flashing the older man his middle finger.

Moriah scanned the deserted beach in both directions before descending from the elevated deck to the patio. It was early in May and too cool for sunbathers and swimmers. Children were still in school, and tourist season didn't start for another week or two. Over the weekend, there had been a few body surfers in the water and several people walking or jogging on the beach, but today was a workday, and no one was in sight.

She checked the driveway and the street and saw nothing or anyone out of place. Sighing with relief, she returned to the patio. Like most beach houses in the area, this one was built on stilts, and in combination with the dunes, it had avoided flooding during the worst of storms over the past sixty years. Ducking under the house, she crab-crawled her way over to one of the middle supports and knelt down. The sand didn't seem to have been disturbed since she checked it the day before. Digging with her hands, she uncovered a black nylon gym bag and pulled it part of the way out of the hole. Unzipping the bag, Moriah stared at the contents. Cash. Cold, hard cash. Almost one hundred thousand dollars. She still couldn't fathom that much money. The money her family had been killed for, and the reason she was on the run.

Brushing back her tears, she took several hundred-dollar bills from one of the many bundles, zipped up the bag, and buried it again in the hole. She tried to make the sand look untouched in case someone glanced under the cottage. Stuffing the money into her back pocket, she crawled out to the patio again. Looking around and still seeing nothing amiss, Moriah brushed the sand off her jeans and hands before heading back into the house.

She decided that after lunch, she would walk the seven blocks to Main Street and the general store to pick up a few things. Not too much, because when she eventually left Whisper, she didn't want to be bogged down with extra baggage. She was positive the money wasn't marked—it was doubtful drug dealers would do that sort of thing—so there was no way she could be traced by using it. The money was one of the few things keeping her alive, and she intended to stay that way.

While preparing a peanut butter and jelly sandwich, Moriah heard a car pull into the driveway and the engine cut off. She knew who it probably was, but she was still wary. Peeking out the kitchen window, she saw KC climb out of a shiny, black Dodge Charger. The car fit the man—sleek, dark, and sexy. A few moments later, as she was pouring a glass of milk, she was startled when the back door suddenly opened and KC walked in. The man walked so softly that she had never heard him come up the steps to the deck. Moving over to the table with her lunch, she sat down, trying hard not to look distressed, as he entered the kitchen.

"Hi." She figured, at least, she could try to be nice, even though she was asking him to leave. "Did you get everything straightened out with your uncle?"

"Yeah, well, about that . . ." He paused, looking everywhere but at her.

Uh-oh. This doesn't sound good.

"It appears I have nowhere else to go at the moment. Everyone's sofas are either already taken or out of service."

"But . . . but you can't stay here," Moriah stammered, beginning to feel like a broken record. There was absolutely no way she could let him stay with her—only if hell froze over.

Holding his hands out to the side, he gave her a pleading expression. "Look, I know you didn't plan on having a room-mate, but I'm only here for a few weeks, and then I'm gone. Back to work. I'll stay out of your way and give you money for the utilities and food." He kept talking as Moriah stood, shaking her head. "I promise I'll clean up after myself, and you won't even know I'm here."

She almost laughed in his face. There was no way she couldn't, and *wouldn't*, know he was there. All sexy, six foot five, 220 pounds of him. All solid muscle. Top it off with hair she was dying to touch and smoldering eyes which seemed to see straight through to her soul every time he looked at her. No, she would definitely know he was there.

"I can even help you out."

At that, Moriah stopped shaking her head and eyed him curiously. She nibbled on her bottom lip for a few seconds, wondering what he was talking about. "How?"

A devilish grin spread across his handsome face as if he knew he'd found a chink in her armored resolve. "Uncle Dan told me about your ex and how you're running away from him. The gun is good to have for protection, but if you get caught without it, how do you plan on defending yourself?"

As much as she hated to admit it, he did have a point. Without that gun, she was helpless. "I hadn't really thought of that."

He tilted his head and narrowed his eyes. "Do you know how to shoot that thing, anyway? You were holding it right, but it didn't look natural in your hands."

"A gun is supposed to look natural?" She let out a very unladylike snort. "That sounds like an oxymoron."

The corner of KC's mouth twitched in amusement. "If you know what you're doing and practice enough, it becomes natural after a while. I can give you a few lessons and show you some self-defense moves in exchange for the spare bedroom." He paused. "I also have a good ear if you care to talk about anything."

Moriah stood silently for a minute, mulling over what he was offering. She could actually use the training. If the people chasing her found her, she had no experience fighting for her life. Hell must be having a blizzard warning because she straightened her shoulders and looked him right in the eyes. "The ear I don't need. The lessons I do. You have a deal as long as you respect my privacy while you're here."

"Deal. If you want, we can start training right after you have lunch."

Moriah nodded in agreement, but inside, she was wondering if she just made the second biggest mistake of her life.

Chapter 6

A huge, black and white sign stating, "Big Al's Gun Shop and Firing Range," hung above the brick building KC parked in front of. The place was nestled between a tattoo parlor and a seedy strip joint. The surrounding, run-down area wasn't much to look at, but it was, ironically, one of the safest parts of town since most of the local cops and residents in the military were members of the range.

Big Al's was twenty minutes and two towns west of Whisper, but it was the only place with an indoor shooting range within a fifty-mile radius. You had to be a registered member to use the range. However, you were allowed to bring one adult guest at a time. Uncle Dan and his three nephews had remained members even though KC and Sean had moved from the area. The membership came in handy when they were in town visiting. They'd had many target-shooting matches over the years, and although his nephews were all expert marksmen and a lot younger than he was, Dan Malone prevailed as the winner more often than not. It was a skill he had perfected long ago in the Army and maintained as he aged.

Glancing at Maura, KC took in her apparent nervousness. "Are you ready for this?"

She met his eyes and shrugged her shoulders. "I guess we'll find out, won't we?"

"I guess we will. Don't worry. With a little practice, you'll be shooting like a professional in no time."

Her dubious expression said she didn't believe him, but she didn't argue with him. "I'm not worried about that, but is this place safe?"

Climbing out, KC skirted the vehicle to help her up from the low seat. "Trust me, it's safe."

As he escorted her into the shop, he became very aware of her, and it felt natural to be walking beside her. Her hair smelled like lilacs or some other flower, and the scent went straight from his nose to his groin. Maybe if he played his cards right . . .

What in the hell am I thinking? Asshole, you're thinking with your dick and not your brain!

This woman was running from an abusive ex and carried a gun. He didn't need to become any more involved with her than he already was. He would teach her how to defend herself during the four weeks he was here, relax the rest of the time, and then he would be gone. He could keep his raging libido in check for a month. End of story.

Yeah, right, jackass. Keep dreaming.

The inside of Big Al's was quiet, except for the muffled sound of gunfire coming from the range located in the shop's basement. The odor of gunpowder and oil hung in the air, but it wasn't overpowering, and KC breathed in the all too familiar scent.

Al stood behind one of the locked display cases, which were

filled with every type of legal weapon you could possibly buy. Stacks of ammunition and gun cleaning supplies were piled on the shelves behind him. He was about six foot even, 300 pounds—hence his nickname—and appeared to have a permanent scowl on his face. Beside him, KC felt Maura stiffen. He understood her reaction since the man gave the impression of someone you never wanted to meet in a dark alley . . . or anywhere else for that matter. But then Al smiled when he spotted them, and his facial features softened dramatically.

"Hey, KC, my man! I didn't know you were in town. How's it hanging?"

Al extended his mitt of a hand to KC, who gave it a hearty shake. "Great, Al. I'm on leave for four weeks. Just got back last night. How've you been?"

"I'm doing better now that you brought this beautiful little lady in to see me." He waggled his eyebrows toward Maura, who visibly relaxed and smiled at his intentional teasing.

KC leaned down until his mouth was near her ear and lowered his voice to a false whisper, which was meant to be overheard by the big man. "Gotta be careful around Al. He's the world's biggest flirt, and the ladies can't seem to resist his charm. It's a surprise his wife, Theresa, hasn't kicked him out yet."

Maura laughed at his playfulness. "I'll have to remember that."

Bringing his voice back to normal, he gestured with his hand toward the two of them. "Maura, this is Al. Al, this is Maura. She's renting my uncle's cottage."

Al glanced at KC, then back at Maura with a stunned expression. "Really? You must have made an impression on the old man. I've never heard of Dan renting the cottage to anyone but family."

Maura gave him a sassy grin. "So, I've heard. It's nice to meet you, Al."

"Nice to meet you, too, pretty lady." He winked at her. "And for what it's worth, my Theresa knows I'm a bit of a flirt, but I've never strayed. I'm too sharp to screw up a good thing. Now, what can I do for you today?"

KC answered for her. "She needs to get in some practice, so I figured I'd bring her in as a guest."

"No problem there." Opening a drawer beneath the counter, he pulled out a piece of paper and a pen. "Just need you to sign a waiver, and then you can head on down to the range."

Ten minutes later, Maura stood in a cubicle, holding her Smith & Wesson 9mm down range, with her eye and ear protection on, staring at a target. It was in the shape of the head and upper torso of a man and was hanging at a distance of fifteen feet. As he adjusted his own protection gear, KC stepped behind her with his head over her right shoulder. He spoke loud enough for her to hear him over her earmuffs. "We'll start at this distance, and as you improve, we'll increase it, okay?"

"Okay. You're the boss."

KC nearly groaned out loud as his body responded to her nearness. If he took half a step forward, his stiff cock would be nestled against her lower back. And if he bent his knees . . . *fuck!* He shifted to give his hard-on some relief, then forced his mind to concentrate on her training.

"Okay. First things first. Never point a gun at someone you don't intend to kill. Unless you're a sharpshooter with years of experience, it's only in the movies where you shoot to wound someone. And firing a warning shot is also Hollywood in action—in the real world, there's no such thing. Always keep the gun pointed at the ground unless you're aiming at a target. Be aware of who and what is near your target. It'll help keep you from accidentally shooting anyone else, but there are no guarantees." He put his right foot between hers and tapped her sneakers. "Move your feet so they're shoulder-width apart, and put your right foot a little behind your left."

She followed his instructions. "Like that?"

Assessing her positioning, he nodded his head. "Good, just like that. Now, extend your arms straight out with your right hand around the grip. Your left hand goes around and under your right, supporting it. You want your finger to be out of the trigger guard until you've decided to shoot so you don't fire the weapon by mistake."

The gun felt as hefty and repulsive in Moriah's hand as it had the night before. It'd come with the duffel bag full of money, and she'd never fired it . . . or any other gun for that matter. Hell, last night, when KC had come through the door unexpectedly, was the first time she'd ever pulled the firearm out and pointed it at someone. She'd been so relieved when it hadn't gone off accidentally. She wasn't sure if she could ever actually fire the gun at someone and quietly prayed she would never have to find out, but it was a good idea to learn how to use it properly, just in case.

Up to ten people could shoot simultaneously in the underground, windowless range. She felt a little shiver go down her spine as KC stepped closer to her back within the small cubicle that separated them from the three other shooters. She wasn't sure if the tremor was because of his close proximity or the ugly weapon in her hand. His warmth and strength surrounded her as he instructed her how to stand and aim at the target. He smelled of spices and salt air, but the scent was very definitely male and made her a little lightheaded. Even though it was muffled by the ear protection she wore, his deep voice was calm and soothing as he gave her directions. Feeling his breath on the nape of her neck, her body let go of another involuntary shudder.

"Are you okay? You're shivering."

Moriah didn't trust herself to speak, so she just nodded. She tried to concentrate on his instructions, but her mind wandered again. She wondered if her finger was in the trigger guard when she'd been aiming the gun at KC's chest the night before.

As if he'd read her mind, he reached out and tapped her right hand. "Last night, your finger was along the side of the gun, as it should have been, but your grip was a little off."

KC stepped to the side to eye her stance again and then moved back behind her. Pointing at two small raised pieces with red dots on them at the top of the gun, he explained, "These are your rear sights. You want to line up the small space between them to the front sight and then line *that* up with where you want to shoot. Okay? Now, line everything up, slowly squeeze the trigger, and try to hit the bad guy on the target."

Holding her breath, Moriah did what he told her, except at the last second, she shut her eyes. The gun discharged with a loud explosion and bucked in her hand, causing her to let out a startled yelp. "Shit!"

Behind her, KC put a steadying hand on her shoulder. "Okay, not bad."

Staring at the target, she cried out in dismay. "But I didn't even hit the guy, and I closed my eyes."

He laughed, and she felt the rumbling sound all the way down to her toes, but not until after it swirled around in between her legs a few times.

Concentrate, you idiot.

"No, you didn't hit him, but you did hit the paper target

within two inches of him. Not bad for your first time, considering you shut your eyes. The shot going off is supposed to surprise you, but try not to let the muzzle come up too far. Don't jerk the trigger. Take a deep breath and start to slowly pull the trigger as you let the air out. And don't close your eyes this time."

Moriah lined up the target with the sights again, inhaled deeply, and gradually let the air out of her lungs as she squeezed the trigger. This time, she kept her eyes open, and when the gun discharged, a small hole appeared in the black area at the lower left side of the target.

"I did it!" She bounced up and down on the balls of her feet, yet carefully keeping the gun pointed down range.

KC let out a hearty chuckle at her excitement. "You sure did, but you just winged him. Try it again. Aim at his chest to stop him. If you have to shoot someone, you want to make sure he's not getting back up."

Moriah tried it repeatedly, and after a box of fifty rounds, she'd made more bullet holes in the black part of the target than not. She was so proud of herself that she briefly forgot why she was learning to shoot in the first place.

After making sure the gun's safety was on, and the magazine was empty of bullets, KC directed her to a small work area outside of the range, next to the steps leading back upstairs to the store.

He gathered their eye and ear protection and placed them in the appropriate storage bins. As he showed her how to break down the weapon before cleaning and oiling it properly, he praised her. "See, I knew you were a natural."

She glanced up at him and was about to answer when his smile turned into a frown. "What's wrong?"

KC was holding two pieces of the dismantled gun and staring at her. His expression was accusing and intimidating. "Where'd you get this? The serial number's been filed off."

Fear overcame Moriah, and she tried to swallow, but her suddenly parched mouth wouldn't allow it. She said the first thing that came to her mind. "I sort of stole it from my ex-boyfriend. I swear, I don't know where he got it, but I took it for protection."

She licked her dry lips as he continued to stare at her. Did he know she was lying?

Nerve-racking seconds ticked by, but then his expression eased, and he nodded his head. "Okay, I'm not thrilled about that, but I can understand it. Just do me one favor and keep it hidden. And do not, I repeat, *do not* point it at anyone you don't intend to shoot."

Moriah's shoulders relaxed a little as she tried to smile and push the tension out of the room. "Like you?"

Letting out an exasperated sigh, KC gave her a small smile. "Yeah, like me."

Chapter 7

KC stood on the patio, grilling the two rib-eye steaks he'd picked up on their way home from the shooting range along with a bottle of merlot and a few other groceries. Two baked potatoes and fresh corn on the cob were cooking on the upper rack of the gas grill. He'd offered to cook dinner for Maura in honor of her being such an excellent student.

Ever since they left the range, he'd wanted to talk to her about her ex-boyfriend, maybe help ensure the jackass would leave her alone, but decided to wait until after they had eaten to broach the subject. Her ex must have really done a number on her because she was obviously frightened, and it killed him to see any woman in that condition. Men who hurt women, physically or emotionally, were the scum of the earth and needed a dose of their own medicine. KC just wished he could be the one to administer it to the bastard who'd harmed Maura and put fear into her beautiful baby blues.

He dropped his head back and stared at the sky. *Where the*

hell did that idea come from? He barely knew the woman and already he was prepared to fight her battles for her?

Get a hold of yourself, Malone. Four weeks of self-defense and shooting lessons. Nothing more. Uh-huh, right.

He told the devil on his shoulder to shut the fuck up. Giving himself a mental shake, he reminded himself that this was temporary, and Maura had given him no signs she wanted to play house for the next few weeks.

If he repeated the "self-defense and shooting lessons only" mantra over and over, he could try to keep himself in check, but he knew it would be hard. When he'd been standing behind her at the range, it had taken all his strength not to wrap his arms around her and pull her against him. Her silky, auburn hair was made for a man to run his hands through it, and her body had been created for pure pleasure. He felt his cock twitch as he thought of how her incredible body would feel under his as he touched, licked, and nibbled every inch of her. He groaned aloud at the image of her doing the same things to him.

Again? Back off, Malone! His mind screamed at the horned, red prick on his shoulder holding a pitchfork.

The lady didn't need to be mauled by a guy who'd been without a lover for almost a year. After an abusive relationship, she needed someone gentle, and he knew if he ever got her in his bed, there would be nothing gentle about what he'd do to her. He would attack her like a male lion with its mate, pawing at her as he took what he wanted, leaving them both exhausted and sated. It would be hot, explosive, mind-blowing sex and probably scare the hell out of a woman like Maura.

KC had been involved with plenty of lovers in his past, but no real relationships. After weeding out the SEAL bunnies looking for a status position, he'd found very few women were willing to stay with a man who could be sent on a mission at the last minute. His tours were long, with the team being incommunicado for weeks or months at a time, and there was always the question of when, or *if*, he would ever be back.

So, he hooked up with women who wanted to have a few weeks of mutually gratifying off-the-wall sex, and when they both decided it was time to move on, they'd go their separate ways with no regrets. It had always worked for him in the past, but lately, KC was starting to think of possibly finding someone to settle down with and have a family. If he left SEAL Team Six and became a training instructor, he would be home most evenings, which would be a plus in any relationship.

When he heard the door above him open, he glanced over his shoulder and watched as Maura stepped out. She leaned over the wood banister facing him. "Since it's still warm out, I thought we might eat out here on the deck. What do you think?"

He stared at her for a minute, letting his eyes roam over her from head to toe. She'd showered after they got home and changed into a pair of gray sweatpants and a white, V-neck shirt which showed only a hint of cleavage, but it was enough to make his mouth water.

What's that cliché? The woman could make a burlap sack look sexy.

Her freshly dried hair was down and blowing gently in the light breeze coming off the ocean. Again, he had the urge to run his fingers through it to see if the strands were as soft as they seemed.

He must have taken too long to answer because she frowned. "Or we could sit inside if you want."

KC shook his head to get his brain and mouth working again. "No, no. Out here is just fine."

Her smile lit up her face again. "Great. Then I'll bring out the plates and utensils."

Turning, she sashayed back through the door, and the sight of her posterior was just as exceptional as the front of her—the woman had one damn, fine ass. He groaned again and turned back toward the grill. Reaching down, he adjusted himself for what felt like the fiftieth time since he'd met her less than twenty-four hours ago. This was going to be the longest four weeks of his life.

Moriah placed her fork and knife on the empty plate in front of her and pushed it toward the middle of the table. "That was the best meal I've had in ages." And she meant it. She'd barely eaten her sandwich at lunch, after losing her appetite over the deal she'd made with KC, but now, she felt more relaxed. "Everything tasted delicious. Thanks so much for making dinner. You're an excellent chef."

During the meal, they'd talked about a variety of safe subjects, such as the town of Whisper, the beach, old movies, current events, and even the weather. Moriah had found it comfortable, soothing, and peaceful. Nothing personal was brought up, and she felt almost normal again. She could be anyone she wanted to be right now. Someone free and safe, without a care in the world. No one else would know the difference . . . but she would know, and that was bad enough.

Swirling the wine in his glass, KC smiled at her. "The pleasure was all mine. I love to cook but don't get a chance to do it often."

"Well, I'm glad you had this opportunity, since I benefited from it." She watched as he took a sip of wine, and her pussy clenched as he swallowed and his tongue peeked out to lick his lips. God, the man, was even sexy taking a drink. How the hell was she supposed to concentrate on anything but his body? He was the epitome of male perfection. His muscles rippled whenever he moved, and she longed to run her fingers and mouth over every inch of him.

Moriah blushed at where her mind had gone and searched her brain for something else to talk about. "So, what do you do in the military? Which branch are you in?"

"The Navy. I joined when I was eighteen, two weeks after my high school graduation. I became a SEAL when I was twenty-three."

"Wow, really? That's a big thing, isn't it? I mean, I don't know much about the military, but everyone has heard about Navy SEALs these days. How long have you been one?"

"Twelve years, but I think I'm finally beginning to burn out." He paused, then grunted. "Huh. That's the first time I've admitted that to anyone except my brothers and uncle."

Tilting her head, Moriah eyed him curiously. "Why do you think you're burning out?"

He relaxed against the back of the chair, stretching his legs out under the table. "I guess I'm just getting tired of being in the worst countries in the world, seeing the evils that exist, and fighting the scum of the earth. I can be out of the U.S. for months at a time, and then I stay in my apartment near the base or here when I have some extended time off. I don't own anything except my car. Maybe it's time to retire, buy a house near the base, and settle down. Leave the fighting and secret operations to the younger guys and start training the newbies."

"Younger guys?" she asked, incredulously. She quickly did the math in her head. "How old are you, thirty-five?" KC nodded in agreement. "I'm twenty-seven, so thirty-five doesn't sound very old at all."

"It is in the SEALs. I'm actually the second oldest guy on my team by one year. In my business, you can burn out quickly. Sometimes I'm surprised I'm still there. But leaving my teammates is a big decision. They're like family, and for a lot of the guys, I'm sort of their big brother."

"As I said, I've heard of Navy SEALs, but never knew what they were, besides being this group of tough guys everyone talks about. Well, that and when they're the heroes of romance novels."

He chuckled as he rested his hands and wine glass on his chiseled abs. "Romantic heroes, huh? I've spent weeks in the middle of nowhere with those guys, without showers and other amenities. I can honestly tell you, there's nothing romantic about it."

She giggled, and he continued. "I'll give you a little military history lesson. SEAL stands for Sea, Air, and Land. It's an elite group formed by the Navy under the orders of President Kennedy back in 1962. Most of the candidates who are chosen for SEALs' training wind up dropping out because it's so intense. We go on clandestine operations, which larger or less experienced units can't do for one reason or another. We can be sent in under any conditions or to any location, but a lot of our training and missions involve water of some sort. Usually, it's our way into or out of some foreign country, unless it's landlocked, of course.

"Some of the missions can be over pretty quickly, while other times, we can be out of the U.S. and undercover for months. Our work sends us into countries we're not allowed to mention, and we perform missions that, as far as the rest of the world is concerned, never happened."

"Is that why you don't have a military haircut? Because you were undercover?"

Nodding, he ran a hand through his hair. "Yup. But I can't tell you anything about it. The key to the SEALs' ongoing success is the silence of its members, and it's the reason our teammates are so close to each other. We can't discuss our operations, successes or failures, with any civilians or members of the military outside of our own teams. We use each other as our own personal psychologists for any subject involving our missions, instead of our families, wives, or girlfriends. Unfortunately, some women have problems with it, so a lot of our guys are single."

"Do you have one?"

His brow furrowed in confusion. "One what?"

"You're obviously not married, but do you have a girlfriend?"

Now why the hell did I ask that question?

Moriah gave herself a mental smack on the back of her head. She wasn't interested in him . . . was she? Well, it wouldn't make any difference if she was or not—he would be gone in four weeks, and she would probably be leaving even sooner.

"No," he answered, staring at her intently. "I'm unattached and have been for quite a while."

Moriah swallowed hard under his scrutiny and changed the subject back to something safe. "You sound like you love what you do."

He silently considered her for a few moments longer before answering. "I do, but like I said, I think it might be my time to move on."

"What will you do if you leave the Navy?"

After taking a sip of wine, he shook his head. "Well, I wouldn't exactly be leaving the Navy, just my team. I've been offered a training instructor position at the base in Little Creek. I'd be training the younger guys."

Her eyes widened. "Wow, that's great. I think you would be a fantastic instructor."

"You do? Why would you think that?"

Pointing to herself, she giggled. "Well, look how well you

trained me to shoot today. I couldn't hit the broadside of a barn, as they say, before I met you."

He grinned. "That was easy. I told you, you're a natural."

"That may be, but I still think you're a great instructor." Tilting her chin up, she all but dared him to argue with her further. "You should go for it."

His gaze fell to his wine glass, and he let out a little chuckle. "Thanks. Maybe I will."

"Good. Now that I've given my unsolicited opinion about your career change, let me clean this up."

When she stood, KC started to rise from his chair as well. "I'll help."

"No, I have it." She waved him back to his seat. "You cooked. Besides it won't take long since we only used the two place settings and no pots or pans. I'll put on some coffee."

As she carried the plates and utensils into the house, Moriah tried to push the feelings of domesticity from her mind. This had been the best evening she'd ever spent with a man, but dinner and conversation were as far as it could go between them. Even if she wasn't on the run, she doubted KC would be interested in her. She was eight years his junior and had come from nothing. He, on the other hand, had a career and plans for the future. Her only plan was to still be alive to wake up every morning—not exactly something to attract a man with.

Chapter 8

KC settled into his chair again as Maura cleared the table. After she had carried the plates inside, he stared out over the ocean and thought about what a pleasant meal it had been. It had been a long time since he'd simply enjoyed talking to a woman. Aside from his attraction to her, he felt at ease in her presence, which would make the next four weeks enjoyable—as long as he could keep his dick out of the equation. She was recovering from an abusive relationship and didn't strike him as the type of woman who would go for a short fling, therefore, she was off limits. Or was she? Maybe things didn't have to be temporary. They had four weeks to get to know each other better. Maybe something good would come out of this. Only time would tell.

The temperature outside was beginning to drop now that the sun was setting, but he didn't want this peaceful feeling to end. He stood and headed downstairs to the patio where there was an outdoor seating area surrounding a black, metal fire pit. A nice roaring fire, coffee, and some more conversation would be the perfect way to finish the day. Crouching down, he reached to retrieve a few logs which were kept under the cottage to keep them dry. He heard Maura come back out of the house above him and figured she'd be wondering where he went. "I'm down here."

"Do you want—?" She stopped short. "What are you doing?"

His head snapped in her direction at the sharp tone of her voice, and he found her staring at him with an odd look on her face. She seemed almost . . . well, scared. "I'm just getting some wood to start a fire. I thought it would be nice to sit down here for a bit. Is there a problem?"

Maura shook her head. "Oh, no. I . . . um . . . I just didn't notice there were logs under there." She paused, and then added, "You might want to be careful, though, I saw a snake near there the other day."

"Really?" His brow furrowed in bewilderment as he stood. "That's odd. You rarely see them this close to the beach."

"Well, maybe he got lost."

"Maybe." KC thought he saw a flash of relief in her expression, and it bothered him. He propped his hands on his hips. "What did you want?"

"Huh?"

"When you came out, you started to ask me a question."

She gave him a small wave of her hand. "Oh . . . um . . . yeah. I just wanted to know how you take your coffee. Cream or sugar?"

"Black is fine."

Maura hesitated a moment, still staring at him standing next to the corner of the house before she pivoted and walked back through the door without another word.

"What the fuck was that all about?" KC muttered to himself. He bent down, inspecting the pile of wood and the surrounding area, but nothing looked amiss. Maybe she had seen a snake earlier—while it was rare, it wasn't exactly unheard of. But then he thought back to the filed-off serial number on the gun she had, and a myriad of thoughts went through his brain. None of them good.

Shit. What the hell has Uncle Dan gotten me involved in?

By the time Maura came back outside with two large mugs of coffee, she no longer appeared to be troubled, and KC had a brilliant fire roaring in the round pit. He added another log and then took a seat on one of three small curved couches surrounding the blaze. She handed him one of the mugs, then sat down on the couch to his left, curling her legs and feet up underneath her body. The evening air had cooled dramatically once the sun had set, but the flames from the fireplace were warm, casting a soft, cozy glow over the patio. The sky was filled with countless glimmering stars, and a slender crescent moon sat high on its throne in the east. Thundering waves pounded the shoreline, their roar muffled by the sand dunes, which separated the beach from the cottage. The only other noises were the crackling of the fire and the occasional cry of a seagull. KC knew it didn't get much more relaxing than this.

He took a sip of his coffee. "So, we've talked about me, let's talk about you."

"What about me?" Maura asked, her expression wary.

"I don't know. Tell me what you did before you ended up in North Carolina."

She shrugged and then gazed at the stars above her. At first, he didn't think she was going to answer him, but after a few moments, she sighed. "I had a part-time job at a local pharmacy. It wasn't much, but it was all I could do while going to school to get my teaching degree. I'm one semester shy of finishing, but now . . . it's sort of been put on hold. Maybe someday I'll be able to finish it."

"What do you want to teach?"

Maura smiled, however, he noticed it didn't reach her

eyes. "I adore children, especially the younger, more impressionable ones. I would love to teach third or fourth grade. At that level, they're really excited about learning new things. Their brains are like sponges. They absorb everything and haven't really started to notice the opposite sex yet."

KC laughed. "What difference does that make?"

She blushed and lowered her gaze to the fire. "Well, it's one less thing on their minds, and they can still concentrate on school. Tell me . . . did you care much about school after you started noticing girls?"

Grinning, he toasted her with his mug of coffee, his eyes dancing in amusement. "Good point." He took another sip of the dark brew. "It sounds as if you are very passionate about teaching. You should return to school if you're so close to finishing your degree. There are a few local colleges within driving distance from here. Just have your transcripts transferred to one of them."

"Maybe."

KC thought she wasn't too enthused about the idea and wondered why. He decided not to press the issue for now. "How about your family? Parents? Siblings?"

His gut clenched when sadness fell over her face.

Moriah knew she was wading into dangerous territory with all his questions and should head back to her room, but for some reason, she couldn't force herself to stand. Even worse, she found herself answering him. "I never really knew my dad. He was in and out of our lives a lot until he finally left for good when I was fourteen. As for my mom, sister, and nephew, they died in an accident a few months ago."

If you called being murdered an accident. She shook the morbid thought from her mind.

"I'm sorry, Maura. That must have been awful for you."

The sympathy in his voice ripped through her, and she fought the tears she felt welling up in her eyes. "If you don't mind, I'd rather not talk about it."

"I understand." He waited a few moments before continuing. "Both my folks were killed in a plane crash when I was seventeen. They were taking a vacation, without us kids, for their twentieth wedding anniversary. A hundred and forty-two others were on board. There were no survivors."

Horrified, Moriah gasped and brought her hand to her lips. "Oh, how awful. I'm so sorry."

KC took another sip of coffee and stared at the fire. "Thanks. Anyway, I know how it feels to lose people who are close to you. Uncle Dan took legal custody of my brothers and me until we finished high school. Sean was the youngest, at fourteen, and Brian was sixteen. After graduating high school, we each enlisted into different branches of the military, Sean to the Army and Brian to the Air Force.

"Thank God for my uncle. It took a lot of courage for a bachelor to take in three recently orphaned teenagers. Dan is my father's brother, and at the time, he was the best thing that could happen to us. He became our rock at the worst time of our lives and made sure we lived up to our parent's expectations. We rarely gave him any trouble, but when we did, he straightened us out really quick.

"Dan served in the military, just as my father did, and neither of them took any crap from us as we were growing up. But they also made sure we always knew we were loved. All in all, I think we turned out pretty darn good."

They sat in silence for a few minutes, alone in their own thoughts. Moriah's heart rate and anxiety were still elevated after seeing KC squatting down near the wood pile. She'd panicked, thinking he would find the duffel bag, and blurted out the first thing she could think of. While he'd seemed skeptical at first, she'd been relieved when he changed the subject to something safe.

Huh . . . safe . . . will I ever feel safe again? She doubted it.

KC shifted in his seat, drawing her attention back to him. After he had taken a sip of his coffee, he brought up the one subject she wished he hadn't. "So, tell me about this ex-boyfriend. What was the fucking asshole's name?"

Caught off guard by the question, she gave the first "fucking asshole" name that popped into her head. "Leo Simmons."

Oh, my God!

She couldn't believe she just gave KC the name of her sister's drug-dealing boyfriend. How could she be so stupid? She had to end this conversation before she said something that would get her in trouble. "I'm getting tired. I think I'll head up to bed and read for a while."

When she stood, ready to run upstairs, KC also got to his feet. "I'm sorry, Maura. I didn't mean to upset you."

Moriah held up her hand to keep him from saying anything more. "It's okay. I would just rather not talk about the past. Thanks again for dinner. I'll see you in the morning."

He watched as she turned and headed for the stairs. "Hey, Maura?"

Pausing, she glanced over her shoulder at him but remained silent.

Sympathy filled his eyes. "I just wanted you to know that I think you're doing fine. You're a strong woman. I'm sure everything will work out for you."

She couldn't tell him how wrong he was, so instead, she nodded. "Thanks, KC. Goodnight."

"Goodnight."

Chapter 9

B lood. Oh God, so much blood. Splattered across the room. On the floor, the walls, the furniture. Crimson red blood everywhere. The raw stench of death hung in the air, surrounding her like a thick, suffocating blanket. What happened? Momma? Susan? Nicholas? No! Oh God, no! They can't be dead! This can't be happening! Why? Oh God, why? It's my fault, all my fault. I killed my family. They didn't deserve to die this way. They're all dead because of me. Run! Hurry! Run before it is too late!

Moriah woke up terrified, covered in sweat, and gasping for air. She fumbled for the lamp next to her bed and turned it on, her gaze darting around the room.

The beach cottage.

She was at the beach cottage in North Carolina—not her family's Chicago apartment—and the walls here were pale blue, and the carpet was ivory. Not dark red. Not covered in her family's blood. There was no lingering metallic odor, just clean, salty ocean air. Momma, Susan, and Nicholas weren't tied to kitchen chairs, sitting there with dead stares and riddled with bullet holes, the souls already drained from their mortal bodies.

Sitting up, she wiped the tears from her eyes and cheeks. Her grief was just as strong now as it had been the exact moment she'd found her family in the apartment and then fled. Would she ever be able to think of them again and not picture how they died? It was all her fault. Well, mostly her fault. She could never forgive herself for the part she played in their deaths. If there was an afterlife, she hoped her family would forgive her. However, she would always blame herself.

Focusing on the small alarm clock on the nightstand, she sighed with frustration. It was five-thirty in the morning. She would never fall back to sleep at this hour, not with the gruesome images of her family occupying her thoughts.

Slipping out from under the covers, she stood, pulled on a clean pair of jeans, and fastened them under the navy-blue T-shirt she had slept in. Stepping into the attached bath-room, she made use of the toilet, flushed, then washed her hands and face at the sink.

As she stared at her reflection in the mirror, she noticed her face was thinner and paler than usual. With the dark circles under her eyes, she could pass as one of those "before" advertisements for some amazing new beauty cream. She hadn't slept more than five hours a night in months, and it was taking its toll on her body. She refused to try an over-the-counter sleeping pill because she didn't want to be groggy if she suddenly had to run again. They had managed to find her twice, and both times she had been able to escape —barely. Learning from her mistakes, she adapted as best she could.

Walking barefoot, she exited the bedroom and went down the hallway into the kitchen. She moved on tiptoes so she wouldn't wake KC. A little coffee and some fresh air would help vanquish the terror that always accompanied the nightmare. She just wished she could find something that would erase the ghastly visions from her mind permanently.

A few minutes later, with a coffee mug and granola bar in hand, she headed for the back deck. Closing the door behind her with a soft click, she turned and jumped in surprise. KC was climbing the stairs in a pair of cotton shorts, a T-shirt, and sneakers. Despite the chilly morning air, his body was drenched in sweat. And what a body it was. His T-shirt clung to him, and she longed to run her hands across the taut plains of his torso and down to his muscular thighs.

A flush of arousal hit her, and she felt a pang of desire low in her belly. She tried to keep the huskiness out of her voice, but she wasn't too successful, and she prayed he didn't notice. "Hi, where were you?"

Halting at the top of the stairs, he grabbed the towel he must have left on the railing earlier and wiped his face and neck. "I couldn't sleep, so I took my morning run a little early."

She was unable to tear her hungry gaze away as he dragged the towel up both of his strong arms. Her mouth watered. "You . . ." Clearing her throat, she tried again to speak. "You look like you just ran a marathon."

Hanging the towel around his neck, he shrugged. "Nope, only ten miles. Five out, five back."

Moriah's mouth hung open as she gaped at him. Had the man actually just run ten miles? *Holy shit!* Well, at least now she knew how he kept his perfect male physique and squeezable ass.

KC shrugged his shoulders again and chuckled. "That's a short hike in the military."

Her eyebrows shot up. "If you say so. I'd hate to think what you would call a long hike. I'd have a heart attack before I finished the first mile."

"*Nah*, not if you did some training." He grabbed a bottle of water he'd also left on the railing and drank most of the fluid before removing it from his lips.

Her eyes flared as his throat worked to swallow every drop. How the hell did the man make drinking look so damn erotic? She dropped her gaze to the wooden deck. "Thanks, but I think I'll pass. I have enough training to do between the range and the self-defense lessons you promised me."

"We'll start those right after breakfast if you want." He tilted his head and eyed her curiously. "What about you? What are you doing up so early?"

She averted her eyes from him, instead, glancing out toward the ocean. "I had a nightmare."

"Oh? About what?"

Moriah refused to look at him as she told him a blatant lie. "I really don't remember."

He stepped toward her, and her eyes shifted back to his face. "Maura, I meant what I said yesterday. I'm an excellent listener if you want to talk about it."

A small, sad smile spread across her face. The man was really nice, and she wished she'd met him under different circumstances. "Thanks, KC. But this is something I have to work out alone."

Sighing in evident frustration, he bent his elbows and flashed his palms at shoulder height as he backed off. "Okay, but if you ever do want to talk, I'm here. I also have some pretty big shoulders to cry on, if you hadn't noticed."

His light teasing at the end was probably an attempt to lighten her mood. She nodded her thanks and shuffled past him toward the stairs. As she descended, she felt his eyes on her and silently cursed the universe for introducing her to a man she could never have.

KC reluctantly allowed her to walk away before heading inside the house to take a shower, shutting the door behind him with a click. He was grateful Maura hadn't asked him why he hadn't been able to sleep. He would have lied because there was no way he could tell her that every time he closed his eyes, he dreamed of her naked in his bed. Their legs twined together, their skin slick with perspiration, and his hands and mouth touching every place on her body he could reach.

He wanted to bind her hands to the headboard and bury his face in her pussy. She would have no choice but to enjoy as he licked, nibbled, and tormented her to an explosive orgasm over and over again. And when she was sated beyond her wildest dreams, he would finally thrust his shaft deep inside her. Not only inside her pussy but her mouth and ass as well. He wanted to take her every way he possibly could and then start all over again.

He'd been surprised to see her awake at this hour. When he found her standing on the deck, he had to force his eyes to remain on her face after he noticed she wasn't wearing a bra under her T-shirt. The fleshy orbs had called for him to take them in his hands and tease them until she begged for more. He'd felt his cock twitch and reached for the bottle of water he'd left out, hoping the cool water would keep him from embarrassing himself with a woody in his sweats. If that happened, she wouldn't be able to miss it under the cotton material. But as she walked past him on the way to the stairs, her unique scent went straight to his groin, and he hadn't been able to stop the lengthening of his cock.

But by the time he reached his bathroom, he'd worked himself into a frenzy, thinking of what she looked like under her clothes, and was harder than he could ever remember being. Turning on the water, he stripped off his clothing and stepped into the shower stall. He needed some relief if he was to face her again without a hard-on.

Grabbing a bottle of body soap, he squirted some in his hand, then wrapped his palm and fingers around his aching cock. He tightened his fist and dragged it up and down while he closed his eyes and replaced his hand with her mouth in his mind. She'd be kneeling before him, her fingers digging into his ass as she clutched his hips. He'd grasp her hair in his hand and tighten his grip until she felt a sting of pain and her juices flowed from her sweet pussy. Her mouth would open, and she would take him inside, her plump, pink lips closing around him and her tongue licking him.

His hand pumped faster, as in his mind, she moaned around his flesh, and the fantasy vibrations did him in. With a gasp and groan emanating from him, his cum erupted from his body in waves until he was finally depleted. Leaning against the shower wall on his other hand, he slowed the motion of the one still wrapped around his ebbing erection. When his breathing returned to normal, he moved under the spray of water to begin cleaning himself off.

Fuck! It was going to be a long four weeks. And that was becoming an unwanted mantra.

Chapter 10

The next three days flew by with a comfortable companionship developing between the pair. In the mornings, they would head down to the beach, where KC proceeded to show his trainee some simple self-defense moves. He adjusted them to take into account her small stature but made sure she could do some damage and give herself time to escape if she ever needed to. The sand was soft and the perfect place to spar because if she ended up on the ground, she wouldn't get injured. Moriah proved to be a fast learner and continued to impress him. With repeated practice, she was able to perform a few of the techniques with almost flawless precision after such a short time.

Their afternoons were spent at the firing range, where he began to increase the distance to the target. He also showed her how to shoot from a kneeling position and from behind cover, drilling into her the importance of showing as little of her body as possible to be a smaller mark. After she had practiced with her right hand, he had her switch the weapon to her weaker, left one, teaching her how to compensate in case her dominant hand became incapacitated.

Moriah threw herself into the lessons and not only amazed KC and herself with her accuracy but also Al, who spent some time observing their practices. He loved to tease and joke with her. "I hope I never run into you in a dark alley."

Moriah giggled. "That's exactly what I thought about you the first time I met you. But now that I know you better, I think you're a pussy cat."

Both men had snorted loudly in amusement over her comment.

While she was grateful KC was teaching her how to defend herself, she was also thankful she was so exhausted by the end of each day. She'd managed to sleep seven straight hours the past two nights without any nightmares, which had shocked her when she awakened feeling refreshed and energetic.

As busy as their days were, the evenings were slow and pleasant. They took turns cooking and cleaning and enjoyed some lively conversations during and after dinner. She was growing comfortable having KC around and, oddly enough, felt as if they had become a couple. Well, at least a couple who had never kissed or even touched each other. Not that she would mind. *Shit no!*

No matter how much she fought her attraction to him, she would love for him to drag her into his arms and kiss her for hours until they both had their fill. She yearned to peel off his clothing, piece by piece, slowly driving him insane for her touch. The more time they spent together, the more she felt her body respond to him. While she couldn't deny she was physically attracted to him, she was pretty confident the attraction was one-sided. KC hadn't made a pass at her or even hinted at the fact that he found her desirable. She had known other women who wouldn't have let the fact deter them and would have shrewdly made their interest known. But Moriah had always been shy when it came to men and sex. Although she had lost her virginity long ago to her high school sweetheart, she had never been the aggressor in any of the few relationships she'd had over the years. Most of them hadn't lasted long. Her boyfriends seemed to tire of always being the ones to initiate sex with her and often left her for a bolder type of woman. One such boyfriend had thrown that fact at her while breaking up with her, and she had felt utterly humiliated.

The problem was she didn't know how to seduce a man and initiate sex, and she was too embarrassed to make any clumsy attempts. Hell, she didn't even know what an orgasm felt like—at least, she didn't think she did. She needed to find a man who would be willing to teach her things, to help her find out what pleased her, and to show her what pleased him. What would please KC? Would he be a patient lover? Would he be willing to show her some moves in bed the way he was showing her when they were training?

Moriah sighed, probably not. KC was an adventurous type, who almost certainly wanted the same from his lovers, and she didn't know how to respond in a seductive way. And it made her feel ashamed of her involuntary faults.

Thursday evening was warmer than it had been for the past week. Dinner consisted of a delicious linguine primavera, which KC had made from scratch. When Moriah complimented him on his culinary artistry, she was surprised to see the macho-looking man blush slightly. He might have been self-conscious, but she thought it was sweet.

Coughing, KC changed the subject. "It's a beautiful night. Are you up for a walk on the beach after dinner? I always feel the need to move around after I eat pasta for some reason. The carbs, I guess."

Not wanting the evening to end, she nodded as she swallowed the food she'd been chewing and then dabbed her mouth with a napkin. "Sure. That sounds nice."

After they had completed the meal, KC cleared the table as Moriah tackled the pots and dishes. Silently she marveled at how quickly they had fallen into a domestic rhythm. She had never lived with any of her boyfriends before and hadn't had a man in the house since her father had left when she was young. It felt odd, yet comfortable, to be living under the same roof as this strong, handsome man who constantly had testosterone-charged vibes emanating from his solid frame. Not for the first time, she wondered what it would be like to caress his sinewy arms, chest, and back. Would he moan at her touch? Would his muscles quiver as he begged for more?

"Are you going to scrub the Teflon off that pan?"

Moriah started at the deep voice just over her right shoulder. Mortified at being caught in a daydream about the man, she quickly rinsed off the sauté pan and placed it on the drying rack. "Sorry, I just zoned out there for a second. Must be the carbs."

Chuckling, he tossed the sponge he'd used to wipe the table into the sink. "Well, now that everything is clean, are you ready for a walk?"

"I think so. Just let me grab a sweatshirt in case it gets too cool before we get back."

Five minutes later, they were strolling down the beach on the edge of where the waves peaked on the sand, propelled by the low tide. The sky was dark, but a faint orange and yellow ribbon from the last of the setting sun still lingered in the west. The moon hung high overhead, giving them enough light to avoid stepping on shells or the occasional dead crab that had washed ashore. They were both barefoot and had rolled their pant legs up a few times to prevent them from getting soaked in the gentle surf. While not frigid, the water was cool, but it was easier to trod on the packed wet sand than further inland where the sea rarely reached.

They traveled in peaceful silence for about a half mile before KC suddenly stopped and grabbed Moriah's arm, forcing her to a standstill.

"Wha—"

"Look! A shooting star," he exclaimed.

Following his pointed finger over the dark blue ocean, Moriah was excited to see a celestial light speeding across the night sky. They both stood in awe at the sight until it disappeared into the horizon.

Moriah exhaled a breath she didn't notice she'd been holding. "Oh, my God. I've never seen a shooting star before. It was incredible!"

KC grinned. "I've seen a bunch of them, but I still find it really cool to spot one."

They began to make their way down the beach again, yet Moriah continued to glance up, hoping to see a repeat of the phenomenon. "Does that happen here often? I've lived most of my life in the city where you're lucky just to see the stars through the smog."

"I've seen a few here. Mostly I've seen them when the team's been on ops overseas."

It was then she realized this was the furthest she'd ever been from Chicago, while he'd been all over the world. "What's it like?"

KC turned his head toward her with a furrowed brow. "What's what like?"

"Being in a strange land. Fighting the bad guys and risking your life for your country."

His broad shoulders shrugged, briefly drawing her attention. "I don't know. I never really thought about it that way before. It's just my job. Someone's got to do it, right?"

"I guess so." Moriah got the impression he wasn't too keen on the subject, so she changed it. "We've gone quite a bit. Should we turn around and start back?"

Without answering her, KC lightly took her elbow and did an about-face toward the direction of the cottage. Moriah's heart raced at the gentle, innocent touch. She wondered if he felt the electricity that seemed to spark down her arm to her fingertips. She didn't know if she was disappointed or relieved when his hand dropped back down to his side. She silently chastised herself. *Get a grip. The last thing you need is an attraction to this man.*

By the time they reached the cottage, she almost had herself convinced.

The next morning, Moriah was sitting on the couch, tying her sneakers, when she heard KC emerge from his bedroom. He wore his usual training-on-the-beach wear, black sweatpants, and a military green T-shirt, yet he was as sexy as ever. His hair looked as if he'd just run his hands through it after his shower, following his routine morning run. He had shaved, and his face was so smooth, she ached to reach out and touch him to see how soft his skin really was. He approached her and seemed oblivious to her wayward thoughts. "All ready?"

"Yup."

"I thought maybe tonight, instead of having dinner here, we could meet my uncle at Sassy's. It's a great little restaurant in town. We've been going there since I was a kid. Sassy's real name is Sara Parnell—a very nice lady. Her daughter and son-in-law took over after Sara retired.

Tonight is their famous 'Friday Fish Fry Night', and I try not to miss it when I'm in town. And, no, I don't suggest you try to say that ten times fast."

The laughter he could bring forth from her often these days filled the room. "I'll take your advice, and that sounds great, especially since tonight is my night to cook."

He let out a little snort. "Well, truthfully, I wasn't looking forward to doing the dishes either."

Feeling more carefree than she had in months, she followed him out the door and down the steps to the patio. A short, wooden pathway threaded its way through the dunes and out to the beach. Striding halfway to the water before he turned around to face her, KC explained that he would approach her from behind and grab her as if he were an assailant. He wanted her to use everything she had been taught in the past few days to escape from him.

He glanced up and down the beach. "Just making sure no one is around. I wouldn't want anyone calling the police, thinking that I'm attacking you for real."

Her smile fell briefly before she could recover. Thankfully, he didn't notice. "No, that would definitely not be a good thing."

More than he could possibly know.

Chapter 11

It was beautiful out, and KC felt more relaxed than he had in a very long time. With each passing day, he was more convinced the reason was the woman standing before him.

Positioning himself behind Maura, he wrapped his right arm around her neck and his left around her waist, pulling her against his chest. Her ponytail was just below his chin, and he could smell the floral-scented shampoo she used. He still didn't know what the name of it was, but every time she was near, the aroma tantalized his nose and warmed his blood, driving him halfway to insanity.

She felt so soft against his hard body. He wished he could grind his pelvis into her ass and nuzzle her neck. Would she let him or push him away?

KC didn't know how badly she'd been affected by the mistreatment she received from her ex-boyfriend. He did know many women had difficulty being intimate with another man after leaving an abusive relationship, depending on how much physical and emotional damage had been done. A lawyer he'd dated for a few weeks several years ago had volunteered part-time at a woman's shelter and told him a few horror stories of the anonymous clients she saw there.

Pulling out of his daydream, he realized they were still standing there, facing the ocean, with his arms draped around her. Was she breathing as fast as he was? Was her heart racing double-time like his? He couldn't be sure. He did know he wanted to stay this way for a while and just drink her in, but it was undoubtedly asking for trouble.

"Uh, Maura?" he asked, trying to control his body's response to being so close to her.

"Yes?"

Was her voice huskier than it had been a few moments ago? He knew his was and cleared his throat. "Are you waiting for something, or is there a reason why we're just standing here?"

"I, um, was waiting for you to tell me to start fighting you."

A sarcastic grin spread across his face. "Do you think an attacker will tell you when it's okay to start resisting?"

"Well, when you put it that way . . ."

She never finished the sentence as she began using her hands, elbows, feet, and even the back of her head to escape him. Caught almost entirely off-guard, KC nearly had his nose broken as she reared up in his arms and threw her head back toward his face. She employed every trick and technique he had taught her over the past few days. Trying to avoid getting hit by her flying limbs, he stepped backward and tripped over a piece of driftwood that had escaped his notice. Losing his balance, he fell backward, and because his arms were still around Maura, she was pulled down with him. He shifted his body so she wouldn't get injured, and she landed on top of him as he hit the sand.

She quickly turned over to face him but remained draped across his upper body. His eyes were closed, but he heard the panic in her voice. "Oh, my God, KC! Are you okay? Are you hurt?"

He made a strangled noise which was a mix of laughing and moaning. "Just my ego. Listen. Do me a favor, will you? Do not, under any circumstances, *do not* tell my team or my family I was taken down by a woman who is barely half my size, or I'll never hear the end of it."

He opened his eyes and found her face a mere six inches from his. She was smiling, but her eyes were still filled with concern for his well-being. He inhaled sharply as he gazed at her soft, pink mouth. Her body stilled. His eyes flickered toward hers, then returned to her mouth as her tongue darted out to moisten her lips. Slowly lifting his head toward hers, he paused. When she didn't retreat, he cupped her cheeks in his hands and crushed his mouth to hers. It took a moment or two, but then her tense body softened against his hard one. He kissed her as if his life depended on it and let out a growl when her lips parted, granting his tongue entry.

Moving one hand to the back of her head to hold her in place, he skimmed his other hand down her neck to her back and then even lower. Wriggling her torso, Maura tried to get closer to him, and KC felt his cock harden immediately. He wanted to strip her naked and take her right here, but it was the middle of the morning, and anyone could walk by any minute now. Knowing they should stop didn't mean he did because the kiss seemed to take on a life of its own. She matched every sweep of his tongue with one of her own. Her taste was like sunshine—crisp, clean, with just a hint of spice —and it was as close to heaven as he had ever been.

He rolled, taking her with him until their positions were reversed. Her hands stroked down his torso and delved under his shirt. He groaned at the contact as electricity coursed through his body, making him harder than he'd ever been in his life. His hips bucked almost involuntarily into hers. She gasped and then moaned. Clutching her hips, he ground his erection against her mound. The woman was burning him alive, and he wasn't sure if he would survive.

A dog's bark in the distance broke through KC's consciousness, and he slowed his exploration of her mouth until he finally pulled away. He stared at her through heavy eyelids. Her eyes were dilated, uncontrolled passion raging in them. Her lips were red and swollen, her ponytail in disarray. He knew he had never seen a woman as beautiful and seductive as this one before him now.

The dog barked again, and both their heads turned toward the noise. Further down the beach was a family of four and an exuberant Collie strolling in their direction. KC didn't think the parents of the two young children would appreciate a sex education display on the beach, and he rolled to his left. Laying on his side so his back was to the approaching family, he faced Maura. She was still out of breath from their brief encounter, and he could see she was as disappointed as he was that it had reached an incomplete end so hastily.

He hoped she would want to continue what they had started later in the day. But for now, he glanced down at his tented sweatpants and then back at her with a devilish grin. "I think I better take a quick swim. Otherwise, I'll look really funny walking around like this."

Her feverish blush was adorable. "I . . . I think that would be a good idea."

Grasping her hand, he brought her palm to his lips. Giving it a quick kiss and a swipe of his tongue, he let it go, then jumped up and ran to the ocean. Not bothering to remove his clothes, he barely paused to toe off his sneakers before diving into the cold surf, allowing it to temper his raging desire and throbbing cock. All the while wishing he could have done it in a more pleasurable and satisfying way.

On the way home from Big Al's that afternoon, they stopped in town to invite Dan Malone to dinner. While KC strode toward the hardware store, Moriah veered off to the little boutique a few doors down. At the shooting range, she realized all her clothes were sweats, jeans, T-shirts, and sneakers —none of which were decent enough to wear out to dinner. They were just the basic necessities for a frightened woman on the run, but with KC's help, she was beginning to feel stronger and safer with each passing day.

There was no way anyone could ever trace her to this little town, which most, if not all, of Chicago had never even heard of. Maybe she could settle here for a while and find a job that paid off the books—it would be too risky to use her real name and social security number. Unfortunately, that also meant she couldn't finish her degree under an assumed name.

Stepping into Petals Boutique, she decided to find something dressy and fun, as long as it wasn't too expensive. While her duffel bag held a significant amount of money, she couldn't spend it on a bunch of frivolous purchases in case she needed it for an emergency. But even though they weren't exactly going on a date, she wanted to find something KC would be pleased to see her in. Something that would turn his head.

Neither one of them had mentioned the fiery kiss they'd shared on the beach, but she had been hyper-aware of him for the rest of the day—more so than usual. Every innocent or deliberate touch had sent an electrical current surging through her veins. And then there were the little looks they kept giving each other. She felt like she was back in high school, and she and the cute new boy were trying to work up the nerve to talk to each other.

She always considered herself a poor flirt, but her body had a mind of its own when it came to KC. It automatically began to move in a mating dance she had never known the steps to. She wanted to stoke the fire they'd ignited on the beach and prayed he wanted that too.

She was lost in her erotic thoughts when a striking older woman emerged from the rear of the store. In her late fifties, she had the brightest eyes and the most beautiful, flawless skin Moriah had ever seen on another woman. "Hi there. I'm Bonnie Whitman. Can I help you with anything?"

Smiling at the woman, she gave her a little hand wave. "Hello. I'm looking for something to wear on a date tonight, but it's not really a date."

Bonnie laughed. "How is a date not really a date?"

"Well, his uncle is coming with us."

"Ah, and three is definitely a crowd." Her eyes sparkled, and Moriah decided she liked the woman's amused attitude. "Well, then, let's see what we can find for you. You're what? A size six?"

She nodded in astonishment. "Yes, how did you know?"

"Honey, I've owned this shop for twenty-two years. I can guess most women's sizes just like that." Bonnie snapped her fingers, emphasizing her statement, then led Moriah to the middle of the shop.

"This area over here is more for your age. I don't cater to the teenagers, but I do carry a variety of styles for the twenty and thirty-something crowd, although most of my clientele is a little older." She quickly pulled three cute dresses from the racks and handed them to Moriah. "Why don't you start trying these on? If you don't like any of them, we have plenty more. The dressing rooms are in the back and to the right."

As Moriah entered the first stall, Bonnie stood outside it and continued to chat with her. "I take it you are Ms. Maura Jennings."

What the hell? Moriah stuck her head out from behind the curtain in utter surprise and tried not to sound rude. "How did you know that?"

"Dan Malone and I go way back." Bonnie waved her hand in a manner that implied Moriah didn't need to worry that people were talking about her. "He married my best friend a long time ago. After Annie died, we remained close friends. I know pretty much everyone in Whisper, and Dan told me he had an attractive young woman renting the beach house, so I just assumed it was you when you walked in."

Relieved a little, Moriah relaxed and stepped back into the small booth, closing the curtain behind her. Undressing, she raised her voice a little so Bonnie could still hear her. "I guess that's Annie in all of those pictures at the cottage. I wondered who she was and why there were only photos of her as a young woman."

"She was only twenty-four when they wed, and Dan was a few years older. They had two wonderful years together before cancer took her from him."

Pulling a dress over her head, Moriah felt sad for the man who'd been so kind to her. "She was so young. That's heartbreaking."

"That it was. Dan never remarried, even after all this time."

Moriah stepped out of the dressing room wearing a navy-blue sundress with a matching short bolero jacket that stayed open over the sweetheart neckline.

"Oh, honey," Bonnie exclaimed as she clapped her hands together. "That dress was made for you. It fits you to a tee and brings out those gorgeous baby blues of yours. KC will be knocked off his feet when he sees you."

Not surprised the woman knew which Malone brother she was interested in, she blushed as Bonnie just chuckled. After picking out a pair of sandals and a small purse to go with the dress, Moriah paid and thanked Bonnie, then took her packages out to the car where KC was waiting.

He opened the passenger door for her. "All set?"

"I think so," she answered with a smile as she sat down on the leather seat before reaching back and placing the bags behind her.

"Great. My uncle said he would meet us at Sassy's at seven, which gives us plenty of time to shower and change." KC shut the door, and she watched his muscular legs, trim hips, and luscious ass as he strode around the front of the car to the driver's side. Her mouth watered, and she was anxious to see how the evening would end—hopefully, how she wanted it to.

Chapter 12

When Maura stepped out of the bedroom, KC was waiting for her in the living room, wearing a pair of khakis with a white button-down dress shirt. He froze and stared at her, his gaze growing hungry and possessive as it roamed over her body in a sensual caress. This was the first time he'd seen her with makeup on, and while she didn't really need any, it made her eyes even more seductive. Her hair was down from her usual ponytail, and he loved how it framed her face.

It didn't escape his notice when she started to shiver under his silent scrutiny, and he smiled to ease her tension. Swallowing hard—twice—he then cleared his throat. His voice was husky with a hint of awe and a lot of appreciation. "You look very nice."

Yeah, that's putting it mildly, Malone. Couldn't you think of a better compliment than that? Stop thinking with your dick and try to come up with something better than 'very nice.' "I mean, you look beautiful . . . exquisite."

"T-thank you. So do you." Maura's face tinged with pink. "I mean, very handsome, not beautiful . . . um . . ."

He loved it when she blushed like that and briefly wondered what other parts of her body would color the same way under his perusal.

Fuck, it's going to be a long evening.

On the ride into town, he could barely keep his eyes on the road as they kept being drawn to the exposed skin of her legs. He prayed Uncle Dan wouldn't want to sit around too long after dinner having coffee and his usual slice of apple pie. KC knew exactly what he wanted for dessert, but it was definitely not on Sassy's menu, and he wanted it all to himself.

As he escorted her into Sassy's Restaurant at 7:00 p.m. on the dot, KC stayed close to her, with his hand splayed across her lower back, leading her to the hostess stand. After he had introduced Maura to Rebecca, they followed the owner/hostess to their table, where his uncle was already seated, waiting for them. KC nodded and said hello to several people along the way but never took his eyes off Maura for more than a second or two. She was absolutely gorgeous and sexy as sin.

When she'd first appeared wearing that knockout dress, he had wanted to say to hell with dinner and ravage her right then, but it'd been too late to cancel on his uncle. Unfortunately, he would have to wait before following through with the wicked ideas which filled his head at the mere sight of her. Feeling a twitch in his pants, he realized, not for the first time this evening, that if he didn't bring his boiling blood down to simmer soon, he would be uncomfortably rigid throughout the entire dinner.

Arriving at their table, KC reached over and pulled out a chair for Maura as Dan stood like the gentleman he was. Over the years, the Malone boys' parents, and then their uncle, had instructed them how to treat a woman properly. They were always taught to open a door, pull out a chair, walk a lady to her door, and stand when one joined them at a table or was introduced to them. If he or his brothers ever failed to do one of those things, they would have received a sharp reprimand or evil eye as a reminder.

Settling back into his chair, Dan Malone smiled at Maura. "You look absolutely beautiful tonight. Whisper seems to agree with you."

She gave him a shy smile in return. "Thank you, Mr. Malone. And I think you're right—Whisper definitely agrees with me."

The older man winked at her. "You're old enough to call me Dan or Uncle Dan. Mr. Malone was my father, and he's long since passed away."

"Okay. Dan it is then."

Their waitress arrived to take their orders, and they all agreed on the "Famous Friday Fish Fry" dinner, which consisted of fried catfish served with hush puppies and coleslaw. KC hadn't been lying earlier—it was his favorite meal to order here. The large platters of food were completed with a few lemon slices, tartar sauce, and malt vinegar, and he had yet to find another restaurant that cooked the catfish even close to Sassy's special recipe.

Before their waitress left to turn in their dinner requests, KC also ordered a round of on-tap dark ale supplied by a local brewery after making sure Maura was okay with the selection. The menu recommended it as the perfect brew to accompany the Friday night special.

Despite the full house, it wasn't long before their dinners arrived, and he was happy to hear Maura found the food and drink to be as delicious as he'd hoped she would. Good conversation flowed throughout the meal as she relaxed and appeared to be really enjoying herself for the first time since her family had died.

Dan and KC both made a conscious effort to stay off the

subjects of her family and ex-boyfriend, and the older man had been more than happy to entertain her with tales of the young Malone brothers. Some of the stories were downright embarrassing for KC, but it didn't bother him. He loved to watch Maura smile and enjoyed hearing her laugh as she listened to his uncle's recollections of their youth.

After their table had been cleared an hour and a half later, Uncle Dan refused coffee, saying he had to get up early to do some errands. But he told them they were welcome to stay and have a slice of Sassy's apple pie for dessert without him. When the waitress returned with a to-go order of pie, his nephew stopped Dan from retrieving his wallet, saying the tab was on him, and then the couple bid him goodnight. KC knew his uncle was playing matchmaker again—he had seen the twinkle in the man's eyes when he rose from the table—but this time, he didn't mind at all.

After Dan had left, Maura's gaze met KC's, and she smiled. "Thanks for bringing me tonight. I had a wonderful time, and your uncle is such a sweet man. The woman, Bonnie, at the boutique told me he's been a widower for a very long time. It's a shame he never found love again."

He nodded in agreement. "Dan always said Annie was his true love, and he never expected to get that lucky twice in a lifetime. But I've always hoped he would find another woman who he could grow old with."

The conversation lulled as they sat there and simply contemplated each other. KC took in her appearance for at least the hundredth time that evening. There wasn't a woman in the room who could compete with her. After a moment, Maura cleared her throat and inquired in a husky voice, "Shall we, um, get dessert?"

Heat flared in KC's eyes and groin. He most definitely wanted dessert, but not here. "Why don't we get it to go?"

After paying the bill, KC had practically dragged her from

the restaurant and was now having a tough time maintaining the thirty miles per hour speed limit posted throughout Whisper. If he had his way, they would be breaking the land-speed record to reach the cottage.

Glancing over at Maura several times during the eight-block trip, he noticed her hands were gripped tightly together as she stared out the windshield. She hadn't said a single word since they'd left the restaurant, and he hoped like hell he hadn't scared her with their hasty exit, but he couldn't wait to be alone with her. He desperately wanted to taste and touch her again, but this time, he wanted to be where they didn't have to worry about being on public display.

Reaching over, he tugged her left hand gently from the grip of her right and brought it to his lips. He tenderly kissed her palm before impishly nipping at her skin. Her gaze traveled from his mouth to his eyes, and she grinned at his playfulness. He was certain his heart stopped beating at that exact moment before it picked up its pace again, this time pounding frantically in his chest.

There was no denying she was beautiful, but it was more apparent when she smiled because her face lit up and her eyes sparkled. He was amazed anyone would abuse such an incredible woman and swore that if he ever met her ex, the guy wouldn't live more than five seconds.

Pulling into the white pebbled driveway adjacent to the beach house, KC turned off the car lights and ignition. Shifting slightly toward Maura, he released her hand and stroked her cheek. His hazel eyes zeroed in on her blue ones. He watched her pupils dilate, leaving only a thin border of sapphire surrounding them. She inhaled sharply at the contact as his hand continued upwards toward her hair. He threaded his fingers through the soft strands. Several stray wisps of auburn silk brushed against his wrist and forearm, causing his breath to hitch. Damn, what he wouldn't give to have her hair draped over his thighs as she sucked him into her mouth and leisurely tortured him.

Cupping the back of her head, he slowly pulled her toward him. The first kiss was a brief feathered touch, but it immediately sparked a fire in his loins. He kissed her again, and this time, his mouth took possession of hers. She whimpered as the kiss deepened, and he responded with a moan from deep within.

Their lips parted, and tongues dueled with each other for dominance. Her hands and fingers traced the contours of his chest and shoulders before reaching around to his back. Her nails dug into his flesh, and he reveled in the pain. Maura tried to inch closer to him, but the seat console proved to be an unmovable obstacle. He realized her dilemma and reluctantly pulled his lips from hers.

Through his heavy breathing, his voice was strangled. "Come to bed with me? Please?"

Without hesitation, she responded in her own husky voice, "Yes."

Fuck! That one word had his cock weeping with need. They quickly exited the car, and he grasped her hand, leading her up the deck stairs and into the house. Using his foot to shut the door behind them, he swung her around and pinned her against it with his body, immediately taking control of her mouth again. Every swipe of his tongue matched one of her own as she wrapped her arms around his neck as if hanging on for dear life.

Setting his hands at her waist, he slowly stroked his way up her sides until his palms brushed the outer surfaces of her breasts. He heard and felt her gasp as his thumbs flickered over her hard but covered nipples. More blood surged to his groin in response. His hands then moved in opposite directions, one to the nape of her neck, the other down to cup her ass, as his pelvis rocked against hers.

KC was getting dizzy with desire and willed himself to slow down, or he would take her right there against the back door. She deserved better than that for the first time he fucked her raw, but Maura showed no sign of wanting to slow down. Instead, the pace of her mouth and hands increased, urging him to follow. Her fingers were threaded in his hair, and the tips forcefully held his head where she wanted it, at just the right angle for her tongue to plunder his mouth.

Never breaking contact, he turned and clumsily walked them toward the hallway leading to the bedrooms. He halted their progress a moment to take her purse from her shoulder and tossed it on the back of the couch.

They paused at the closed door to his bedroom, and he fumbled to find the knob, reluctant to stop touching her to do so. When the door finally swung open, he backed her into and across the room. The back of her legs hit the bed, and he felt her body stiffen. A jolt of worry zapped through him, and he pulled away from her mouth to look down at her flushed face. "Is something wrong?"

Maura lowered her eyes to stare at his chest. "No . . . yes . . . I mean . . . I don't know."

Placing his hand under her chin, he gently forced her gaze back up to his curious eyes. "You don't know?"

Her hesitation bothered him until she opened her mouth and stammered, "It's . . . it's just that I . . . I'm not really good at this."

Confused, he shook his head and took a step backward. "What are you talking about? Maura, honey, from what I can tell so far, you're excellent at this. I could kiss you for hours."

"Not kissing." Her gaze fell to the carpet, and her voice dropped to a mere whisper. "I mean the . . . the sex part."

His eyes narrowed as he studied her face. She was serious. "What are you talking about?"

She sighed and shrugged her shoulders as her cheeks reddened with obvious embarrassment. "In the past, I've been told that I'm not that good in bed, and I don't want you to be disappointed."

KC's jaw tightened with anger at the thought of any man telling Maura she wasn't good enough at anything, much less having sex with her in the first place. "What fucking asshole said that?"

Not waiting for an answer, he took her hand and guided it to his hard and throbbing cock. "This is what you do to me, just by looking at me. Sweetheart, sex goes both ways. Maybe things weren't right because the selfish jackass didn't take his time to show you how good it could be."

Leaving her hand at his groin, he trailed his palm back up her body to her breast. "No one took the time to find out what made your body respond in pleasure." He rubbed his thumb over her peaked nipple, and she inhaled sharply. "That's how you make sex good—great even. Let me show you."

Maura arched her back, her eyelids fluttering closed as he continued to rub the ripe bud through the thin material of her dress and bra. She gasped, then sighed, her body closing the distance between them as if pulled by a string. "KC, show me. Please show me how good it can be."

He growled. "With pleasure, honey. With absolute pleasure."

Chapter 13

K C took her mouth again, and she melted in his arms. Moriah wanted him in a way she had never wanted any other man. She grew bolder as they kissed and found her hands reaching out to KC, seemingly without an order from her brain. Gripping his sculpted shoulders, she pulled him tighter against her own body.

Never had she responded to a man this strongly and quickly before. Inhaling him, she reveled in running her hands over his solid form. Her blood was boiling, and she felt moisture flush from her pussy. The throbbing between her legs beat in time with her racing heart. She couldn't believe her body's reaction to KC. In the past, it had always taken plenty of foreplay for her to be even half this responsive. Her body was ready to take him, and they were still fully clothed.

Gathering the material of her dress in his hands, he pulled it up her body and over her head, one slow, excruciating inch at a time. Normally, she would be self-conscious of a man undressing her, but all she felt with KC was heat, electricity, desire, and passion.

He tossed her dress aside, then ran his calloused hands

over the soft, smooth skin of her shoulders and back, trailing down to her buttocks, which he grabbed and squeezed. She desperately wanted his clothes and the rest of hers to disappear until there was nothing between them—skin on incredible skin.

He must have read her mind. Leaving her mouth, he nuzzled her neck at the spot just below her ear. "Undress me, sweetheart."

Backing up half a step, he gave her room to get her hands between them so she could unbutton his shirt. This was a first for her. The guys she'd dated in the past had always undressed themselves before hopping into bed with her.

After she had finished with the last button, her hands stroked up his torso and burrowed under his shirt. How could his skin be so soft yet so hard at the same time?

God, she wanted to lick him.

Taste him.

Devour him.

She'd never felt this alive before, this empowered, and she didn't want the feeling to end.

Pushing the shirt off his shoulders, she let it drop to the floor and lowered her hands to attack his belt buckle. All the while, KC kissed and nibbled on her shoulders and neck. Having trouble with the buckle and not being able to look down with his head in the way, she had to beg him. "Please, help me."

He didn't stop what he was doing, but his hands went to his waist, and within seconds, he had the annoying accessory open. Instead of undoing the button and zipper of his pants himself, he returned her hands to them so she could do it for him. It didn't take her long, and she shoved the khakis from his hips, revealing his black boxer briefs. KC kicked off the pants, then made fast work of removing her bra and underwear.

Picking her up in his arms, he skirted the bed and placed her in the middle of the mattress. Lying beside her, he started to bestow more kisses on her body as if he were worshiping her. His mouth slowly worked its way down her neck to her shoulder and then further to the valley between her breasts.

His hands seemed to be everywhere at once, heating her flesh as they caressed her waist, hips, back, and legs. He stroked her outer thigh and then torturously began a slow advance to the pulsating heat between her legs. The torment was so intense she wasn't sure how much she could take before begging him to touch her where she needed him the most.

His hand stopped at the crease of her hip, and simultaneously, his thumb flicked her clit as his tongue swiped her nipple, and she nearly jolted off the bed. "Oh, God!"

KC didn't break his stride as he continued the thrilling assault on her body. He pulled the stiff peak of her nipple with his lips and teeth before giving the same attention to its twin. His deft fingers found her labia soaking wet as he stroked her, matching the rhythm of his mouth. She squirmed and tried to get closer to him. She wanted him inside her . . . now!

"Not yet, sweetheart," he murmured into her skin. "Just relax and enjoy."

"C . . . can't . . . mmm . . . more! Please!"

KC smiled against her skin. "Oh, there'll be more, my sweet. Plenty more."

His fingers still stroking her, KC's mouth began a painstakingly slow journey down her torso, pausing briefly to lick her navel as he shifted lower on the bed. Kissing her hips, he settled himself between her knees and paused, staring at her wet sex. Moriah felt embarrassed by his scrutiny. Another first—she'd never had a man just stare at her pussy while licking his lips. "What's wrong?"

"Absolutely nothing. You're so beautiful." He lifted his gaze to hers, and she blushed at the heat she saw there. He glanced back down to where his fingers continued to softly caress the curls of her pussy hair. "I knew when you blushed, you would turn pink all over. God, how I fucking love that."

KC brought his mouth to her clit and gave it the same attention he'd laved upon her nipples. Moriah struggled for breath as her back arched off the bed, and her hands gripped the comforter. She gasped and rolled her hips, trying to get closer to his teasing mouth. "KC! You're killing me!"

She felt him laugh against her swollen folds, the vibrations taking her higher. "No, I'm not, sweetheart. I'm pleasing you and enjoying every minute of it."

Involuntary moans escaped her as two fingers breached the slit of her weeping vagina. Her body instantly yielded to the invasion, and with one more swipe of his tongue over her clit, Moriah experienced another first—she climaxed for the first time in her life. Until now, she'd thought she was incapable of having an orgasm.

She screamed her release. A bright, white light blinded her, even though her eyes were shut, as a flood of pleasure she never knew existed washed over her. Fucking her with his fingers, KC let her ride out the violent storm, but before she fully recovered, he lowered his mouth to replace his fingers. His stiffened tongue penetrated her as his thumb brushed over her clit, sending her over the edge of another incredible orgasm and making her quake uncontrollably. Her response scared and elated her at the same time. This was beyond anything she could have ever dreamed of.

This time, KC allowed her to come down from her orgasmic high. As Maura lay breathless, he reached over and retrieved a condom from the nightstand drawer. Shoving his briefs down his legs, he kicked them off while using his teeth to rip open the small package and swiftly sheathed his throbbing dick.

Crawling up her body, he stopped to hover above her. She looked beautiful and sated, but he was far from done with her. "Open your eyes, honey."

Her lashes lifted, exposing the blue eyes he could drown in and die a happy man. Reaching down, he lined his cock with her slit. She was so incredibly wet, making his entry easier. Her hips tilted upward as he slid in and out of her, going further with each pass. She grabbed his upper arms and dug her nails in as KC eased himself into her, filling her. She was so tight, he worried he might be too big for her. "Are you okay, baby?"

"Yesssss—" Her hiss was cut off by a gasp as his pelvis tapped her clit on an inward thrust. She shifted her hips again, pulling him further into her moist heat, and KC groaned. Her walls were as snug as a glove, and the drag of his cock against them was killing him. He lost all control and slammed into her.

Tucking his face in the curve of her neck, he nibbled the spot over her pulse. He had wanted to take things slowly for her, but his body had other plans. Quickly finding the right pace to make her moan and scream again, he pounded into her as she matched him thrust for thrust. He didn't know how long he could hold back his own orgasm, but he desperately wanted her to come one more time.

Increasing the tempo, he felt her begin to shudder. As she climaxed again, her inner walls tightened around him. With his own guttural cry, he came with such force he thought he might pass out as wave after wave of ecstasy hit him.

Resting his head against her shoulder, he tried to regain his breath, and from what he could tell, she was having the same trouble. Reluctantly, he slowly withdrew from her and rolled to her side. The cool air in the room felt good against his fevered body, slick with perspiration. Not wanting to leave her, he sat up, removed the condom, tied it off, and tossed it in the trash pail next to the nightstand. Laying back down beside her, he smiled as she cuddled up to him and murmured, "So that's what I've been missing."

A minute later, she was sound asleep in his arms.

KC awoke on his left side, spooning the woman who lay beside him, her back to his chest, his arm wrapped protectively around her waist. He pulled her closer and inhaled her scent. It was a distinct smell—female, flowers, and sex—but it was all Maura.

They had made love twice more during the night, but he still woke up hard and wanting her again. If he lived to be a hundred and had her every day, he didn't think he would ever be satisfied.

Checking the bedside clock, he noted it was 8:00 a.m. That was the latest he'd slept since his second night in the house. As much as he wanted to wake Maura slowly and fill her again, he knew she needed some sleep. The only other thing he could think to do was run off his excess sexual energy.

Easing himself away so that she wouldn't awaken, he climbed out of bed and headed to the bathroom to relieve himself. A few minutes later, dressed in his usual running shorts and T-shirt, he left her a quick note with a pen and paper he found in a drawer of the nightstand.

Didn't want to wake you. Went for a run. - KC

With his socks, sneakers, and a towel in hand, he left the bedroom, closing the door as quietly as possible. He made a fast pitstop in the kitchen to grab a bottle of water from the refrigerator. Exiting through the back-porch door, he found his brother Brian sitting in a chair with a cup of coffee, staring at the ocean. "Hey, bro! Good to see you. Why didn't you knock or let yourself in?"

Brian was two years KC's junior and the spitting image of their mother. With his brown eyes and dirty blond hair, he'd won his senior class yearbook category of "Best Looking"—a fact he never let his other brothers forget.

"Uncle Dan suggested you might need some extra rest." He smirked. "Guess he was right."

Knowing his brother was aware of Maura's presence and had figured out their uncle's attempt at matchmaking, KC ignored the man's sexual snark. Sitting in one of the deck chairs, he went about putting his socks and shoes on, leaving the towel and water on the table. "Want to take a run?"

After swallowing a sip of coffee, Brian shook his head. "Nah, I already did five miles this morning. I'll just relax and wait for you to get back."

"Suit yourself."

"I always do." And wasn't that the truth?

KC started out at a steady pace along the edge of the surf. He felt exhilarated this morning, and it had everything to do with the woman he had left in his bed. He doubted she fell into bed with just anyone—her lack of experience and shyness had all but proven his theory—and he considered himself incredibly lucky to have been one of the few.

They'd spent much of the night exploring each other from head to toe. There were areas of her body that, if touched or kissed, made her gasp. Other areas made her moan. And one or two even made her scream. He grinned at the thought. She had screamed in delight many times during the night, and he couldn't wait for a repeat performance. Yup, he definitely was a lucky man.

An hour later, he returned to find his brother exactly where he left him. Brian tossed him the towel. "Your lady friend hasn't come out yet. She too . . . *ahem* . . . worn out to join us?"

He growled. "Watch it, asshole."

Leaning back in his chair, Brian propped his feet up on another one. "So, tell me about this mystery woman Uncle Dan rented the cottage to."

Wiping the sweat off his face, KC shrugged. "No mystery. Maura was in an abusive relationship. When she'd had enough, she took off running. She's just afraid the jerk will come after her, so she's keeping a low profile. Uncle D. felt sorry for her and decided to rent her the house."

"Uh-huh."

He didn't like the skeptical response. "Come on. You know Dan. Always bringing home strays."

Tilting his head, Brian conceded . . . a little. "Of course, but this is the first time you ever became involved with one of those strays."

His eyes narrowed. It wasn't like his brother to stick his nose in any relationship either of his siblings got involved in. "I won't deny I'm attracted to her, but I've only known her less than a week. Who knows where this is headed? For now, I'm enjoying myself, and so is she. No harm, no foul. So back off."

Brian held up one hand as a sign he was doing as requested. "Okay, bro. I just don't want you getting involved in someone else's troubles."

"She left those troubles behind her."

The door behind him opened, and they both turned to see Maura emerge from the house, oblivious to their conversation. KC grinned at her rumpled state, but she looked rested and incredibly sexy. She had thrown on a pair of black sweatpants and a gray T-shirt. Even though he could tell she wasn't wearing a bra, KC knew Brian would never embarrass her by mentioning it or indicating in any way that he was aware of the fact. He had grown up learning the same gentlemanly traits KC had.

When Maura noticed KC wasn't alone, her gait and smile faltered. Both men stood, and he took care of the introductions. "Brian, this is Maura Jennings. Maura, this is my brother Brian. He's a detective with the State Bureau of Investigations out of Elizabeth City and lives about forty minutes away in Camden."

At the mention of his career, Maura paled slightly but quickly recovered. KC may not have noticed, but Brian definitely did, and it piqued his curiosity about the woman even more.

Studying her with the eye of an experienced detective, he stepped forward and held out his hand. "It's a pleasure to meet you."

She cleared her throat and, after a moment's hesitation, shook his hand. "It's nice to meet you, too." He noticed her swallow hard under his gaze, and she tugged her hand from his. Struggling to smile, she turned to KC. "I'm going to make some coffee—do you want some?"

Wanting to look around inside without either of them there, Brian spoke up. "Why don't I make it? You two sit and relax." He pointed at a paper bag sitting on the table, which he'd brought with him earlier. "I picked up some bagels and scallion cream cheese for breakfast. I'll bring out plates and utensils too."

Not waiting for either one of them to turn him down, he

made a beeline for the door. Inside the cottage, he quickly set the coffeemaker and then gathered some plates, knives, and napkins and placed them on a serving tray. As the coffee brewed, he glanced around the kitchen, not seeing what he was looking for.

He moved on silent feet back into the living room. Spotting a small purse on the back of the couch, he glanced toward the porch. Making sure KC and Maura couldn't see him, he quickly opened the purse and found her wallet. "Moriah Jensen" was the name on the Illinois driver's license next to a picture of Maura.

Huh? Now why is she using an alias? Probably for nothing good.

Memorizing her date of birth, Brian put the wallet back in the purse and left it exactly how he found it. Returning to the kitchen, he poured two cups of coffee and set them on the tray along with the milk and sugar.

Putting on an air of nonchalance, he picked up the tray and headed for the porch door.

Chapter 14

Panic assailed Moriah as she watched Brian enter the cottage.

Oh, God, a state investigator! A cop!

What were the fucking odds KC's brother would be in law enforcement? This could get very ugly, very quickly, if she didn't get herself under control. She couldn't do anything that would raise suspicion, and that meant she had to act as normal as possible, and she did everything in her power to appear unflustered.

Pretend he's a stockbroker, she told herself. *Yeah, right. Good, fucking luck with that.*

KC reached out, took her arm, and pulled out a chair for her. A shiver traveled up her spine as he whispered in her ear, "You look beautiful this morning."

Moriah wasn't sure if the trembling she felt was a reaction to KC or fear. "Th-thanks."

His eyes narrowed as he inspected her face. "Everything okay?"

"Um, yeah." She smiled. "Just trying to wake up. You wore me out last night."

Grinning, he placed a kiss on her lips. "Right back at you."

A noise behind them had Moriah and KC turning, and the latter rushed over to open the door as Brian carried a full tray out. Noting the coffee, KC raised an eyebrow. "Just two cups? You're not having any?"

"No, sorry, Bro. I just got paged into the station. You two enjoy breakfast." He regarded Moriah in a way that made her want to squirm. "It was nice to meet you, Maura."

She prayed neither of them could hear the hammering of her heart. "It was nice to meet you too."

"I'm sure I'll see you soon."

She nodded and told herself not to read into those words. He was just being friendly, wasn't he?

Twenty minutes later, her stomach churning, Moriah sat there, picking at the bagel KC had placed in front of her but never bringing a morsel to her mouth. His brother's visit and fast exit bothered her. She tried to convince herself there was no way he could know about her and her past, but something about their whole interaction left her unsettled.

Devoid of an appetite and needing the think things over, she stood, obviously catching KC off guard. "I'm going back to bed."

"Mind if I join you?" There was no missing the hopefulness in his question.

"I'm sorry, KC, I'm not feeling well." At least, it was the truth. "I think I'm coming down with something. Maybe a nap will help me feel better."

Clearly not happy about it, KC bit his lip and nodded, but she was grateful he didn't push the issue. "Okay, you go rest. Let me know if you need anything. I'll check on you later."

Not wanting him to worry, she leaned down and gave him a quick kiss on the lips. "Thanks."

On her way to her room—not his—Moriah grabbed her purse from the couch. She shouldn't have left it out in the open last night, with her real ID in it, but then again, she didn't even recall how it ended up there after they arrived home. She had been too busy kissing KC.

Closing the bedroom door behind her, she turned the lock, then tossed her purse on the nightstand as she flopped onto the bed.

She couldn't shake her uneasiness about Brian Malone. How could she have been so stupid? How could she have let her guard down? She had been crazy to think she could settle down here. There was no way she could do anything normal again. To do so could end up with her being killed.

Shit! She had just spent the most incredible night of her life with the most amazing man in the world, only to discover he had a detective for a brother. Now she would have to leave sooner than she'd expected, and the thought of leaving KC was tearing her apart. It shouldn't, considering she barely knew him. But it was. She was probably just another conquest in a long line of women he'd slept with.

The thought made her jealous, although she had no right to be, and she chastised herself. Last night was just a one-night stand. He hadn't professed love for her. They had known each other less than a week—there couldn't be love there. That only happened in romance novels and fairy tales, didn't it?

But Moriah knew it was there, deep down in her heart. She had fallen in love with KC the first time he had kissed her on the beach. His touch and scent were forever burned into her memory. She would never forget him. But she couldn't stay and risk her past catching up with her—it would only place him in danger, as well, and she couldn't do that to him. Somehow, she would have to pretend that nothing was wrong for the rest of the day. She couldn't have KC suspecting she was planning on running away. It would create too many questions, and she was having a difficult time leaving him as it was.

Standing, she walked into the adjoining bathroom, used the toilet, then washed her hands. Studying herself in the mirror, she wished her life was normal again and her family was alive. But that wasn't going to happen. She couldn't rely on anyone to keep her safe—she would have to do it by herself. If she told KC what had happened, he might not believe her, or if he did, he could end up being killed when the ugliness she had left in Chicago caught up with her. She was certain one day it would, and she couldn't put KC at risk. The best thing to do was leave tonight. She could already feel her heart breaking.

Reluctantly, she made up her mind. Tonight, after KC fell asleep, she would grab her things, along with the bag of money, and disappear. She could walk into town and call a cab to take her back to the Walmart in Elizabeth City. From there, she would catch a bus to God-only-knew-where . . . just anywhere but here. Pulling the covers up to her waist, she settled into the soft mattress. Now that she had a plan, she would need to get some more sleep. The Lord only knew when she would feel safe again.

Maura hadn't looked at him and had barely uttered a word since his brother left. She'd just sat there, not eating the bagel he'd given her. KC knew she must be regretting last night.

Fuck. He shouldn't have pushed her so hard. But he had wanted her badly and just assumed they were on the same page when she had responded so quickly. Well, he didn't regret last night one bit. It had been the most fantastic evening he had ever spent with a woman. Whoever had told her she wasn't good in bed was a fucking ass. She had been like molten lava in his hands, and he had lost track of how many orgasms he'd brought her to. The woman was incredible in bed, and he was growing hard just thinking about it.

After she had gone back to bed, he sat there brooding for a while. Somehow, he had to change her mind and banish any regrets she had because now that he had taken her to his bed, he was dying for it to happen again. He still hadn't had his fill of her, and he'd be damned if he only had one night with her.

Shaking his head, he headed inside to grab his car keys, cursing himself the entire time.

Two hours later, after an extra-long workout at the local gym a high-school buddy owned and then a subsequent shower, KC pulled into a parking spot in front of the hardware store and turned off the engine. He sat there a moment, drumming his fingers on the steering wheel, again replaying the night before and this morning over and over in his mind. He couldn't think of a single thing he had done wrong except, perhaps, push Maura too fast. Maybe, he should have just waited a few more days. However, at the time, he had wanted her so painfully that he couldn't make himself wait any longer. *Fuck, I'm a jackass.*

Banging his hand on the steering wheel in frustration for the fifth time since he had left the cottage, he climbed out of the car and headed into the shop. His mind elsewhere, he wasn't paying attention when he tripped over Jinx lying in the doorway and ended up sprawled on the floor in front of the counter. The lazy-ass dog picked his head up, gave him a "whatever" look, and promptly went back to sleep.

"Useless, fucking dog," KC mumbled while getting to his feet and brushing himself off.

Dan, who had observed the entire incident from his seat behind the counter, was laughing hysterically. "Don't be mad at him because you can't watch where you're going. What's got you in such a sour mood? I thought you'd be walking on cloud nine today."

Giving the dog a last annoyed glance, KC's eyes narrowed as he turned toward the counter. "Why would you think that?"

"Brian stopped back here on his way out of town." That was all Dan needed to say. KC could figure out the rest on his own.

He shrugged his shoulders. "Apparently, my idea of the morning after differs from Maura's. She barely said two words to me this morning and went back to bed after Brian left. Told me she didn't feel well, but I don't think that's what's going on."

"Shoot, boy, what'd you do wrong?"

Shaking his head, he stuck his hands into the pockets of his jeans and leaned against the counter. "I haven't the damnedest idea."

"Well, then, figure it out, son! I happen to like the little lady a lot, and I think she's good for you. I mean, she's *perfect* for you!"

He gaped at the man. "What? Do you have us eloping already? I've only known the woman a week."

"I'm not getting any younger. Unless I give you boys some help, I'll be waiting forever to become a great uncle. I want to enjoy the little ones while I can. And don't you dare elope," Dan added, pointing his finger at his nephew.

"Holy crap! Not only do you have me marrying her—you have us having kids already? What the fuck, Dan?"

The man sighed. "I know when two people belong together. It was obvious how y'all looked at each other last night that you two were made for each other. Now, go buy Maura some flowers and apologize for whatever the hell you did, even if you don't have a fucking clue what it is."

KC just stared at his uncle as he headed to his office at the back of the store. Shaking his head, the younger man stepped over the snoring canine and walked back out into the bright sunshine. Thinking his uncle might be right, he headed to the florist up the street.

Not long after KC left, Jinx lay in the middle of the third aisle, where he'd moved to continue his nap. But he jumped up, his tail wagging furiously as he trotted over to Bonnie Whitman as she strode through the front door of Malone's Hardware store. The older woman laughed as she bent down to scratch the dog's ears. "Well, hello there, good boy. You always know who walks in with dog biscuits in their pockets, don't you?"

Reaching into her jacket, she pulled out a giant bone-shaped treat. The dog promptly plopped his butt on the floor and offered her a paw. She shook Jinx's outstretched limb and handed him his gift. Even though his mouth was full, the dog gave her a grateful *woof* and retreated to the back of the store with his prize. Behind the counter, where he had been paying some bills, Dan snorted and shook his head at his deceased wife's best friend. "You spoil that dog."

Bonnie smirked. "Oh, and like you don't. Besides, I don't have any grandchildren to spoil yet, so Jinx reaps the benefits." Her only son and daughter-in-law were newlyweds who lived in the suburbs of Washington, D.C. Much to her chagrin, they had put off having children right away. "I hear you've been doing some matchmaking lately, you old coot. How did their date, which wasn't really a date, go last night?"

He grinned widely. "Pretty darn good, if I do say so myself. Dinner was fantastic, and apparently, so was the rest of the evening. They might have hit a small bump this morning, but KC is picking up some flowers to smooth things over. I'm telling you, Bonnie, those two were meant for each other. I can feel it right here." He tapped his hand over his heart. "You know, she reminds me a lot of Lori, the boys' mother, which works out well since KC is the spitting image of his father. It's a shame Tommy never had a chance to know his sons as men. He would have been so proud."

"Just like you are. You did an excellent job with those boys after their parents died, and they love you for it."

"Thanks," he replied sheepishly. "So, what can I do for you, or did you just come in to make my dog fat and me happy?"

As if on cue, Jinx came running back to beg for the second biscuit he knew Bonnie had for him, and she handed it over. "Actually, I came by to see if you could come over to the house sometime in the next few days and take a look at the toilet in the spare bathroom. I want to know if it's an easy fix or if I need a new one before I call the plumber. I don't trust contractors anymore since that electrician tried to cheat me last year. Thank God you came by before I signed anything, and he started working. They think they can get one over on dumb, single, old ladies like me."

Dan scoffed. "You are certainly not dumb, most definitely a lady, and don't look a day over forty. I would be happy to swing by and take a look, as long as you make your famous meatloaf as payment for my professional services."

Grinning, Bonnie winked at him. "You're on. Is tomorrow night okay?"

"Sounds perfect."

After she left the store and headed toward her boutique, Dan returned to his bills and started whistling a silly tune.

Chapter 15

When he returned to the little cottage, KC pulled into the driveway. After much debating, he'd picked out a large bouquet of flowers in various colors. He then decided to make a picnic lunch for Maura. Women loved romantic gestures like that, he told himself, and he'd do anything to get out of the proverbial doghouse.

He'd also stopped at the food mart and picked up some fruit, crackers, pepperoni, and an assortment of cheeses. Then he selected a bottle of merlot at the liquor store and drove home, feeling much better about the day.

Carrying his purchases into the kitchen, he placed them on the counter before searching for a platter to put the food on. After everything had been prepared, he set the meal on the porch table, in addition to a vase filled with the bouquet.

He re-entered the house and strode down the hallway, stopping in front of Maura's room and hesitating for just an instant, suddenly unsure of himself. Knocking softly, he waited for her to open the door. Instead, he heard a soft, "Yes?"

"I made us some lunch. Are you hungry?"

There was no answer for a moment. He didn't realize he was holding his breath until she finally replied, "Give me a minute to freshen up. I'll be right out."

They ate a quiet lunch, verbally dancing around each other, talking about the same safe subjects they had discussed at dinner the first night KC had been there. It was almost as if they had never made love . . . had never rocked each other's world.

He'd hoped the romantic lunch, flowers, and wine would create the closeness they had enjoyed last night, but Maura seemed to want to keep her distance. It was driving him fucking crazy.

Unable to take it anymore, he reached for her hand, which was resting on the table, and placed his own on top of it. "I'm sorry."

Maura's eyes flew open, then narrowed in surprise and confusion. "About what?"

"Last night."

She lowered her eyes to her lap, her cheeks reddening. "I . . . I told you I wasn't that good at sex."

Staring at her in amazement, he scrambled to explain. "No! That's not what I meant." Extending his other hand, he cradled her cheek. "Oh, honey, you were incredible. You absolutely blew my mind. Several times, in fact."

Her blush deepened, and he remembered how the rest of her had pinkened last night and felt himself getting aroused again.

"Then what are you sorry about?"

His thumb brushed softly over her cheek. "You seem so quiet and out of sorts today. I just assumed you were regretting last night. I'm sorry if I pushed you too soon."

She gave her head a slight shake. "You didn't push me. I

wanted you more than anything last night. I-I never knew it could be like that."

Her gaze dropped to the table, and he slid his hand down to cup her chin and lifted it until she met his eyes again. "Then what's wrong?"

"Nothing, really." She shrugged. "I'm just a little embarrassed. I don't have much experience with men, especially someone as nice as you, and I'm not sure how I'm supposed to act, I guess."

He stood and pulled her up with him. As he wrapped his muscular arms around her small waist, he leaned down and gently kissed her lips. Maura sighed and melted into his embrace, thrilling him.

"You don't have to act. Just be natural—relax and enjoy yourself. You don't have to be experienced to do that." He nibbled her lower lip, and she took a small, quick breath. "I like that you're a bit naive, and yet, you're so responsive to me."

He pressed his lips to hers and ran his tongue along the seam, urging her to let him in. Her mouth opened, and he reveled in her taste as his tongue danced with hers. Melon and strawberries teased his palate. Drawing her even closer, he deepened the kiss as the last of the tension left her body. She was so soft against his contrasting, hard body, but she fit him perfectly. Never had a woman completed him as Maura did. It was as if she had been made just for him.

His lips didn't leave hers as he bent down and hooked an arm under her knees. Securing his other arm behind her back, he carried her inside and strode purposely down the hallway to his bedroom. He eased her legs down beside the bed and dragged her against himself. His rigid cock rubbed her abdomen, and he let out a rabid hiss.

He opened his eyes when she pulled away from the kiss and then closed them again as she began to explore his body with her hands. They stroked his shoulders and chest, then slowly made their way down his taut torso. When her fingers delved under the hem of his shirt, he obliged her by quickly pulling it over his head and tossing it to the ground.

His eyes remained heavy, but he watched her through thin slits shaded by his eyelashes. Her hands worked methodically upward again and stopped over his unyielding pectoral muscles, which contracted as if shocked by her touch. She glanced up at him seductively before bringing her mouth to replace her hands. KC growled like a wild animal but stood still and let her continue her tantalizing exploration. His fists were clenched at his sides as he struggled to let her take the lead. Her tongue touched his nipple, and he nearly came at the erotic feeling which shot straight to his groin.

He mimicked the words she had said to him last night. "You're killing me."

Maura smiled against his skin but didn't let up. "As they say, 'what's good for the goose is good for the gander.'"

"If that's the case . . ." He didn't finish as he yanked her T-shirt up her body and over her head. He was almost disappointed to see that, sometime since this morning, she had put on a lacy white bra. His hands cupped her round globes of flesh, loving the feel of their weight in his palms. He rubbed his thumbs over her stiff buds while her hand dove into the front of his increasingly tightened jeans, her fingers finding him stiff and ready. He hissed as she made a fist around his shaft.

Losing his patience with their slow seduction of each other, KC quickly shed his jeans, boxer briefs, socks, and sneakers and then proceeded to strip Maura of her remaining clothes. He gave her a gentle push, and she fell back on the bed before scooting into the middle. She looked so damn sexy, and it was all for him.

Retrieving a condom from the nightstand, he covered himself in latex as she viewed him through half-closed eyes. Stepping between her legs, he grabbed her knees and brought them up to his flanks. Leaning on the bed with one knee between her legs, he trailed his hand up her left calf toward her sweet pussy. Never taking his eyes off her face, he probed her entrance with two fingers and found her drenched and ready for him. Thrusting his fingers in and out, it wasn't long before she was begging him. "Please! I need you! Please . . . oh, God!"

He would have liked to have the satisfaction of making her beg some more, but he couldn't wait any longer. The urge to fuck her until neither one of them could walk was something he couldn't ignore.

Lowering his body to hers, he settled between her wide-spread legs and ran his aching dick through her folds. When he was certain they were both wet enough for her to take him, he thrust forward, and her body yielded to him. He gasped when he was buried to the root, and his balls slapped against her ass.

Knowing this time would be hard and fast, he told himself there would be plenty of time later to make up for it. "Honey, I can't go slow."

She moaned as he pulled almost all the way out and then filled her again. Her fingernails dug into his back. "I don't want it slow."

Thank fuck!

He pounded into her, taking them both up the proverbial mountain and hurtling toward the edge of the precipice. Her tits bounced with every thrust, drawing his gaze. Damn, they were so fucking pretty. Leaning over her with his weight on one hand, he brought the other to her nipple and pinched it, drawing a loud gasp from her. "Oh! Oh, KC! More!"

Pulling out of her, he flipped her on her stomach and

tugged on her hips until she was on her knees, her ass high in the air, while her upper torso rested on the bed. He lined his cock up with her slit again and plunged forward. He fucked her as hard as he could without hurting her. The sounds of flesh slapping against flesh and their combined grunting and gasping fill the room.

She clutched the bedspread in her hands and begged him to send her into ecstasy. Reaching around her waist, he found her clit with his fingers and rubbed the little pearl as fast as he could. Thrusting her hips back toward him, Maura screamed as she climaxed around him. Her tight, quivering walls squeezed his shaft and sent him flying over the edge after her. "Fuuuuuck! Shit!"

He came with the force of a hurricane, shooting his cum in waves inside her, and for the first time in his life, he cursed the protection he wore. What he wouldn't give to know what it was like to be bareback in her hot cunt. Bright lights flashed behind his closed eyelids, and he felt like he was on a dizzying amusement park ride. Their dueling orgasms seemed to go on forever until they finally collapsed in a sweaty, heaving, satiated heap on the bed.

When he had the strength, he slid out of her warmth and rolled to the side. He quickly disposed of the condom and lay back down beside her, pulling her against him. They were asleep within minutes.

They spent the rest of the day and night in bed, leaving only for the occasional food or drink for energy or a bathroom break. Moriah couldn't get enough of the man. She knew she had planned to sneak out that night, but after KC had taken her back to his bed, she couldn't deny herself this one last night with him.

Now at just after midnight, lying next to him as he snored softly, she brushed her hand over his chest and abdomen. She knew from her brief experience with him that if she tried to get out of bed, he would wake up and teasingly pull her back into his embrace. And that, of course, would lead to another round of passionate lovemaking. He was insatiable, and it seemed he'd awakened the sexual beast within her because she couldn't say no whenever he started nibbling on her neck and shoulders. And then, by the time he worked his way down her body and licked her clit, she'd be reduced to begging for him to fuck her over and over again.

Who knew she could satisfy a man as virile as him? Definitely not the woman she'd been a few days ago.

Sighing, she rested her head on his shoulder and felt his arm around her tighten. She would have to make her escape tomorrow. Maybe she could send him into town for something. She worried it was a mean thing to do, running away without warning or an explanation, but she didn't know what else to do. If she stayed here, she would eventually be discovered or, even worse, put KC in danger. She loved him too much to do that, so her only alternative was to run as far away from him as she could.

For now, though, she would make memories to take with her, to comfort her when she was finally alone again. And no matter where she ended up next, she knew she would leave her heart here with him.

Chapter 16

The sound of knocking at the back-porch door the next morning, followed by a loud bark, had both Moriah and KC moaning as they rolled from a mutual embrace and wiped the sleep from their eyes. Moriah glanced at the bedside clock and was surprised to see it was after nine. KC had held her close the entire night, and she'd slept like a baby—another memory to keep for when she was back on her own again.

KC groaned loudly as he sat up and ran a hand through his unruly hair. "Sounds like Uncle Dan."

Not wanting to be caught in KC's bedroom, Moriah jumped up and frantically searched for her clothes. Swinging his feet off the side of the bed, he stood and grabbed a pair of sweatpants from his duffel. "Calm down. He'll wait on the deck for us."

Stopping short, Moriah gaped at him, her face redder than he'd ever seen. Clearly mortified, she almost yelled, "He knows we've slept together?"

"He's hoping we are." KC was mildly irritated at the morning's interruption. He'd wanted to shower with her before treating her to breakfast in town. "He's a bit of a matchmaker. Don't be embarrassed. Uncle Dan is a true romantic and would never make you self-conscious about it."

She nodded, but by the way she was biting her bottom lip, he could tell she still wasn't thrilled with the revelation. KC threw on a clean T-shirt, kissed her sweetly on the tip of her nose, and headed for the bedroom door. "Go ahead and have a shower before joining us."

After stopping in the hallway bathroom to relieve himself, he exited the cottage and found his uncle downstairs on the patio, with a knowing grin on his face. The older man's eyes sparkled with delight. "Hope I didn't interrupt anything? Or did I?"

KC furrowed his brow as he descended the staircase. "Don't be talking like that when Maura comes out. I told her you were a complete gentleman."

"That I am, laddie," Dan replied, using his mother's off-the-boat Irish accent. "So, have you thought about what you're going to do about Team Six yet?"

Sighing, KC dropped onto the loveseat opposite his uncle. "I don't know. As much as I hate to leave my men, I think it's time. I spoke to Admiral Cohen before I left and told him I'd have an answer for him when I returned to duty."

"You'll make a fine instructor."

KC nodded. "That's what the admiral said."

"Then he's a smart man."

Glancing around, KC realized something was amiss. "Where's that mutt of yours? He's usually slobbering all over me or passed out on my feet by now."

Dan surveyed the area. "Around here somewhere. He wouldn't wander far."

He heard a noise and peered into the darkness below the cottage. "Damn dog is digging under the house." Rising to his feet, he strode over and crouched down at the edge of the patio. "Get outta there, Jinx!"

His uncle appeared next to him. "Must have found a crab or something."

The black dog had dug a large hole near the center of the house and appeared to be pulling something out of it. Annoyed, KC climbed under the floor joists and crab-walked to where the dog desperately tried to make the hole bigger. "What the fuck are you digging for dog . . . gold?"

Jinx paused to look up at him with a big sandy grin, then immediately went back to work. KC pushed the dog out of the way and peered into the opening. Seeing black nylon fabric exposed, he brushed away more of the sand. When he realized it was a duffel bag, he grabbed its strap and pulled it from the hole. Pulling back the zipper, he sat down hard and stared at the contents. "Holy, fucking shit!"

"What is it?" Dan asked from the patio.

Dumbfounded, he fingered the banded stacks of bills, which added up to more cash than he had ever seen at one time. Regaining his senses, he started to crawl out with the bag when he heard footsteps on the stairs. Despite being underneath the house, he was still able to hear her. "Hi, Dan. Where's KC? I thought he was out here with you."

Climbing out from under the house, he saw her inquisitive expression turn to one of horror as he stood with the duffel bag in hand. As the color drained from her face, a realization hit him like a punch to the gut—she knew about the money. "Is there something you would like to tell me, Maura? I take it you know about this bag of money. What the fuck is going on?"

"I'll tell you what's going on." All eyes turned to where Brian Malone came around from the side of the house onto the patio. He crossed his arms over his broad chest and glared at Maura with laser-light precision, full of intimidation. "She's wanted for questioning in the murder of her mother, sister, and five-year-old nephew."

"No!"

She yelled at the same time KC and Dan's wide eyes whipped back to her, and the men let out a "what?" in unison.

They all began talking at once until Dan put two fingers in his mouth and whistled loudly to get the others' attention. "Hold it! Everyone calm the hell down! There's obviously a story behind this whole mess." Staring at Maura, his gaze softened—it was evident the man didn't believe he'd let a murderer rent his house. "Maura, did you kill your family?"

He quickly put up his hand haltingly when Brian opened his mouth to interrupt.

"No! Absolutely not! L-Leo did!" She sobbed the words out through her tears.

Confused was a drastic understatement to what KC was feeling right now. "Leo? Your ex-boyfriend?"

"He wasn't my boyfriend. He was my sister's boyfriend."

Sighing heavily, he gestured to the seating around the fire pit. "You've lost me. Sit down and tell us what the fuck is going on."

Maura, Dan, and KC took seats while Brian stood behind his uncle, still glaring at Maura as if he was ready to haul her off to jail, no questions asked. Jinx lay at her feet and, at the moment, was the only one who appeared to be entirely on her side, even though Dan seemed to be more than halfway there. KC dropped the duffel at his feet, then leaned forward, setting his elbows on his knees. He glanced up at his brother. "First things first. Where'd you get this information?"

"Yesterday morning, when you introduced us, I noticed she got pale and scared when you told her I worked for the SBI. You obviously didn't notice. My radar went up. When I went inside for the coffee, I saw her purse and looked at her license, which stated her name is Moriah Jensen, from

Chicago. I went to the station after I left here to run her name but ended up working a road rage turned armed robbery. I was so busy I forgot to run her through the system, so I swung by the station this morning, and lo and behold, I got a hit. Four months ago, her family was shot to death, and she disappeared off the face of the Earth. She hasn't been named an official suspect yet but is listed as a person of interest."

Turning back to Maura, KC tried to ignore the tears welling up in her eyes. Anger replaced his shock, and it took everything in him not to go ballistic on her. "What happened?"

She swallowed twice and tried to regain her composure. Wringing her hands together, she stared at the empty fire pit and told them about the nightmare she had been living in for the past few months. "My name *is* Moriah Jensen. I lived in a three-bedroom-apartment with my mom and younger sister. It wasn't in the greatest part of town, but it was the best we could do after my father took off for good. Susan, my sister, was always hanging out with a bad crowd and getting in trouble, but when she became pregnant, she changed. She stopped seeing those assholes and took care of herself.

"When Nicholas was born, Mom and I helped out as much as we could. Susan found a waitressing job and was going back to school for her G.E.D. Things were going well for all of us. Nicholas was a beautiful baby, and Susan really loved him. We all did.

"Then, about six months ago, I noticed the signs that Susan was using drugs again. I discovered she was dating this local drug dealer Leo Simmons. I was furious and told her I would call Child Protective Services and have Nicholas taken away from her. I don't think I could have done it, but I wanted her to believe I would file a report. Anyway, she promised me she would stop seeing him.

"The day they were . . . were killed . . ."

She paused, took a deep shuddering breath, and released it slowly as the men waited in silent impatience. "That morning, I went into Susan's room to find a pair of shoes she'd borrowed from me. Instead, I found that duffel." She pointed at the bag now sitting on by KC's feet. "Inside were the money and the gun."

She shook her head. "I-I was absolutely stunned. I couldn't believe my sister had brought a gun into the apartment with a five-year-old. I didn't want to wake my mother and upset her because it was her one day off, and she hadn't been feeling well. I thought I could handle the situation on my own. Susan had already left to take Nicholas to preschool, but I knew he would be back at eleven. I didn't want the gun in the apartment when he returned, so I took the bag with me to work. I don't know why. It was such a stupid thing to do.

Glancing at the beach, she took a moment before continuing. "Anyway, I put everything in my locker at work and called Susan around nine fifteen while on my break. We were both yelling at each other. She was angry I took the bag, and I was more livid she had it in the first place. She told me it belonged to Leo, and she swore she didn't know what was in it. He'd asked her to hold it for a couple of days, and as naive as Susan could be, she did—no questions asked. I told her it was drug money and I was going to bring it to the police. She said Leo would kill her if I did. She was convinced he had some connections in the police department."

With tears streaking down her face, she paused again to catch her breath.

"How did she know that?" KC asked quietly.

"S-she had seen a guy at Leo's apartment once and recognized him as a detective who occasionally came into the restaurant with a few other officers. She didn't know his name, though."

He nodded, his jaw tense. "Okay. Go on. What happened next?"

"She begged me to just bring the bag home, and she would return it to Leo. I don't know why, but I finally agreed." Moriah's body was now trembling as much as her voice. "B-but when I got home a little after three o'clock, the door to the apartment was open a bit. I-I went inside and found Mom, Susan, and Nicholas . . . gagged and tied to kitchen chairs. They'd all been sh-shot to death. There was blood everywhere—the walls, the floor, the . . ."

She closed her overflowing, tear-filled eyes as if trying to block out the horrifying memory and took several deep breaths to prevent herself from hyperventilating. Dan shifted over to the seat next to her and took her hand in silent support. She glanced at him and gave a nod of thanks before picking up where she'd left off. "I assume Leo or one of his friends did it. They had wrecked the place, probably looking for the bag. I was about to call the police, but then I remembered what Susan had said about Leo having connections. I didn't know if Susan had told them I had the money before they killed her, so I went into my room, grabbed a few clothes, and ran. I knew they would kill me if they found me, so I left Chicago and started hitchhiking and taking buses. I slept in bus stations and motels if I could find one that didn't ask for ID. I've been on the run ever since. They almost caught me twice."

While KC was still stunned by her story, Brian took over the questioning. "How?"

"Once at the bus depot in Chicago, when I was trying to get out of the city, I saw Leo and two of his buddies searching the station. I slipped out through a service entrance and ran, then hitchhiked out of the city. The other time was about a week later in a small town about a half-hour south of Columbus. I'd gotten a lift from a couple of college girls, and we got into a fender-bender. The police came before I had a chance to disappear. I had to give the officer my ID. I didn't think anything of it at the time because I'd never been on the run before. I stayed at a run-down motel that night, and the next day, I was in a convenience store and saw three guys in a black Escalade cruising up and down the main road. The license plate was from Illinois. I just knew they were looking for me and got out of there as fast as I could."

Brian relaxed his stance a little, but it was clear he wouldn't give her the chance to run even if she thought she could make it past them, which she couldn't. "The cop had no reason to run your license right away, but it was probably entered into the computer when the accident report was filed. That's how they most likely traced you."

Wiping her wet eyes, she nodded, then watched as KC dragged a hand down his face. He didn't know what to believe at this point and wanted to think she was telling the truth now, but that would mean everything before this had all been a lie. He should have known something was up with her, but his heart and his dick had apparently done the thinking for his brain.

Brian came around from the back of the couch, nudged the duffel bag out of the way, and sat next to his brother. "How much money is there, and where's the gun?"

A low whistle came from Dan when she said the amount. "One hundred thousand dollars, minus what I've used to eat and stuff. The gun is in my room."

KC narrowed his eyes and glared at her. "That's why the fucking serial number was removed, wasn't it?" Biting her lip, she nodded, and he turned to his brother. "I was teaching her how to shoot the damn thing so she could defend herself."

Rolling his eyes, Brian stood again and began pacing from one end of the patio to the other. "Oh, great, just fucking great. This just keeps getting better by the fucking minute."

"Is there any way you can find out what's going on up in Chicago . . . you know, without raising any red flags?

KC's brother stopped pacing and put his hands on his hips. "Unfortunately, my inquiry will probably result in me getting a phone call from the Chicago PD sometime today, but I'll say her purse was turned in as found property or something. I'll call Sean and ask if he has any contacts up in Chicago. Maybe he can have someone do a little snooping around."

The youngest of the three, Sean Malone, was an FBI agent in Jacksonville, Florida. Turning to Moriah, he pointed a finger at her. "In the meantime, I'm taking the money and gun and securing them. I can't believe I'm about to say this, but you are to stay here where KC can keep an eye on you while I check out this story. I almost believe you, but I'm also a little wary until I have proof you're telling us the entire truth. And God help you if you're lying because I'm putting all our asses on the line here."

Sobbing, she put her hands over her heart. "I swear, I'm not. I . . . I loved my family and would never have hurt them."

KC stood. While he was pissed off at her, he knew in his gut she was telling the truth about what had happened to her family. What he didn't know was if everything that happened between the two of them had all been a farce. "I believe her, and she'll stay right here with me until we hear from you." He gestured for her to stand. "Let's go get the gun and give it to Brian."

Without saying a word, she nodded solemnly and

preceded him up the stairs. Before the door shut behind them, he heard Brian ask their uncle, "Do you believe her?"

The older man responded in no uncertain terms, "Absolutely."

"You and your damn, fucking strays."

Chapter 17

It was noon when Chicago Police Detective Frank Parisi sat at his desk and turned on his ancient department computer. The CPD was in the process of updating their systems, but until they made their way through every precinct, he had to put up with an eight-year-old unit. With fifteen years on the force, nine of them as a detective in the Homicide Unit, Parisi was used to the department's "hurry up and wait" standard for getting new equipment.

Five more years, and he could retire from this hellhole. Between his CPD pension and the money he had made on a few side ventures, which the department didn't know about, he and his wife, Diane, could live very well in Florida. He could spend his days fishing, and Diane could do whatever the hell she did when he wasn't home. He didn't care what she did as long as he had the freedom to do what he wanted.

A red dot flashed on the computer screen, and Parisi sat up straighter. Glancing around, he made sure no one was in his vicinity and clicked on the alert.

Hallelujah!

After months of being underground, that bitch, Moriah Jensen, had finally appeared on the radar again. They would've had her a few months ago if that hick cop in Ohio had processed the accident paperwork faster.

Scanning the alert, he read that a North Carolina State Investigator, Brian Malone, had run her license. But if that was the case, why the fuck hadn't he called CPD and told them he had her in custody? The whore probably batted her eyes, and the schmuck released her with a warning before he got the BOLO—be on the lookout—request back on the computer. *Fucking idiot.*

Parisi snatched up his desk phone's receiver and dialed the number which was listed on the computer screen for Investigator Malone. When it went to voicemail, he left a message for the asshole to return his call.

Grabbing his jacket, he headed toward the door, advising the unit receptionist he was going to check on a lead and would return later. His partner had taken the week off because his wife had just given birth, so Parisi was flying solo for a few days. It was just as well since his partner was a Goody Two-Shoe who would run straight to Internal Affairs if he knew who Parisi was doing business with. There was no love lost between him and his partner. As long as the guy kept his nose out of Frank's business, the detective could tolerate him.

He drove his department-issued Crown Victoria eight or nine blocks and then turned left into the bus depot. Hurrying inside, he made a beeline to a row of lockers and pulled out his key for unit #702. After opening the door, he pulled out one of the throwaway cell phones he'd been given, which couldn't be traced. There was no way he could risk making this call from his department phone or his own cell phone. After powering it up, he dialed the number from memory as he shut the locker door and headed back outside.

Four rings later, the call was answered by the gruff voice belonging to Adrian Hernandez. "What?"

Parisi glanced around to make sure no one was within hearing distance as he strode across the parking lot to his vehicle. "Guess who's been spotted in North Carolina."

"How, when, and where?"

"Some hick cop down there ran her license in Elizabeth City. I tried to call and see if he had her detained, but I just got his voicemail."

"Let me know what he says."

Parisi wasn't surprised when Hernandez hung up on him without warning as he was used to the rude manner by now. The man was the biggest drug supplier in Chicago and would pay Parisi nicely for discovering the woman's whereabouts. He'd gotten himself assigned to the Jensen murders to help clean up the mess Leo Simmons had caused. That two-bit loser gave his ditzy girlfriend a duffel bag stuffed with money, and a gun, which could be tied to two other murders in the city, to hold for him. *What a fucking ass!* Now the money and gun were missing, along with his girlfriend's sister.

Climbing back into his car, he hoped Hernandez killed Leo when this was over for all the trouble the jackass had caused. He'd be happy to do it for the drug lord. For now, though, he would head back to the station to wait for the investigator's call.

Sean Malone hung up the phone after talking to his brother, Brian. So much for a few days off.

Fuck!

KC and Dan had really stepped into it this time. Opening a file on his laptop, he scanned his law enforcement associates list and found the number for a Drug Enforcement Agency contact in Chicago. He'd worked with the agent during a joint task force case a few years ago and hoped he hadn't been transferred.

He called, and after five rings, Agent John Samson answered the phone. After exchanging pleasantries, Sean gave the agent the rundown on Moriah's story and asked if Samson knew anything about the case or the drug dealer Leo Simmons. He wasn't happy with the agent's response.

Half an hour later, Sean was in his bedroom, packing a travel bag. He had two hours to get to the airport and through security with his weapon before his plane took off from Jacksonville, Florida, to North Carolina. He'd fill his brothers in with the details when he arrived at the beach house. It looked like the Malone boys would ride again and rescue a damsel in distress. *Yee-haw!*

After two hours of waiting for the phone to ring, Frank Parisi was anxious and very tempted to head for the men's room for a snort of the coke he kept in the hidden pocket of his sports coat. The phone rang at the same time he stood. Sitting back down, his hand covered the receiver. Taking a deep breath, he answered the call with what he hoped sounded like a bored voice. "Detective Frank Parisi."

"Hello, Detective. This is Investigator Brian Malone from North Carolina's SBI, returning your call."

"Yes, Investigator, thanks for calling. I received an alert that you ran the license of one of my BOLOs . . . a Moriah Jensen." He grabbed a pad and pen to make some notes.

"Yeah, *um*, someone turned in a purse with that ID in it. I ran it to see if it was stolen property. I thought it was a little odd to find her bag in North Carolina when she's from

Chicago." He paused and then added, "So this Jensen is wanted for questioning in a couple of homicides, huh?"

Shifting his eyes around the room, he kept his voice quiet enough not to be overheard by the few detectives working at their own desks or the conference table in the middle of the bullpen. "Yup. Looks like she killed her mother, sister, and the sister's kid. Shot 'em several times each, then took off running."

The investigator whistled softly over the phone. "Really? Fuck, that's cold. What makes you think she did it?"

Pausing a moment, Parisi narrowed his eyes at the other man's fishing expedition. "Well, like the BOLO says, she's just wanted for questioning. It's a little suspicious she disappeared immediately after the murders."

"Yeah, I guess that would be suspicious. I wonder what her motive was if she did do it."

Aggravated, he leaned back in his chair. "Well, that's something I'll ask her when we locate her."

Malone sighed. "I wish I could help you out, Detective. But I have her picture—I'll pass it around the barracks and see if anyone recognizes her."

"I'd appreciate that, Investigator Malone. If you could put that purse in your property room, just in case we need it for anything, that would also be great, you know, to maintain chain of custody."

"No problem. Anything to help you big-city boys."

"Thanks." His upper lip raised into a sneer while he tried to act as if nothing was wrong. "You have a good day, and let me know if Ms. Jensen shows up anywhere in your parts."

"I'll do that."

"Thanks again." Parisi hung up and muttered, "Dumb, fucking hick."

Within fifteen minutes, he was back in his department vehicle, dialing the same number on the throwaway phone.

After this conversation, he would break the device down into pieces and dispose of them in different trash containers.

Adrian Hernandez picked up the phone on the first ring this time. "What is it?"

"I heard back from that cop in North Carolina. Says someone turned in the girl's purse."

"And?" The man's irritation was clear.

"And I think he's lying." Parisi put the car in drive. Might as well grab something to eat, then find a place to have a quick snort. "I could be wrong, but he seemed a little too interested in finding out what we had on her."

"Yeah? What's his name? I'll send a few boys down that way to see what he knows."

"State Investigator Brian Malone. Called from the Elizabeth City SBI office on East Main Street."

"Got it. If this turns out to be something, you'll have a little extra in your pay this month." Hernandez hung up before the detective could respond.

Hanging up the phone in the quiet report room, Brian ran a hand down his face and let out a heavy sigh. He hated to lie to the detective, but until he got a better idea of how much danger KC's girlfriend was in, he was better off fudging the truth a little. He hoped the guy hadn't recognized he was fishing for information. Thinking back over the conversation, he realized he'd laid it on pretty thick several times.

Probably thinks I'm some dumb hick.

On his hip, his cell phone chimed when a text came through. With a quick glance at it, he was surprised to see Sean's message saying he would be boarding a flight to North Carolina soon and would grab a rental car at the airport. Brian hadn't expected his brother to drop everything and fly home to help, but that's how the Malones were—when one was in trouble, the others came running.

Sean had also left a message for a DEA agent in Chicago, and he'd fill them in later. Sighing, Brian prayed that Maura . . . Moriah . . . or whatever the hell her name is . . . was not about to screw KC over. If she wasn't telling them the truth, they could all be in serious trouble.

The door to the room swung open, and one of the Field Training Officers walked in with a recent academy graduate. Standing, Brian gave both men a nod before heading for the door. His next stop was the District Attorney's office, where he had a meeting scheduled to discuss the road rage/armed robbery incident from yesterday. At least, that would keep his mind off the mess Uncle Dan had brought to the family's door—unintentionally, of course.

Damn that man and his fucking strays.

Moriah sat on her bed in silence, watching KC stalk back and forth across the room. He wasn't just mad, he was furious. She could tell by the heat flaring in his eyes. It wasn't from flames of passion like it had been that morning. Instead, it was as if his brain was about to spontaneously combust unless he calmed down.

Jeez, had it only been two hours since they had made love?

Finally, he stopped pacing and stood before her with his arms crossed over his broad chest. She swallowed hard as his eyes pierced hers, but she refused to look away. He had a right to be mad, and she deserved his wrath.

"So . . . do I call you Maura or Moriah?" Oh, yeah . . . he was pissed. His anger was barely leashed.

She shrugged, and her gaze wavered, then dropped to his

chest. "You can call me Moriah. It doesn't matter now. You know who I am."

"Do I?" She flinched as he spat out the words. "Apparently, I don't know a damn fucking thing about you!" The volume of his voice got louder with each word. "You lied to me. You fucking lied to me from day one! And after we fucked around, you continued to lie to me!"

"I'm s-sorry," she sobbed as she pulled her knees to her chest and wrapped her arms around them. "I was scared. I-I didn't know who I could trust. I was afraid of what would happen if I told you the truth."

He recoiled like she'd slapped him in the face. "How could you . . . how could you sleep with me if you didn't trust me?"

His voice had dropped to almost a whisper, and she didn't know if that was better or worse than the yelling. "No! It wasn't like that! I swear!"

His eyes narrowed until the veins at his temples bulged. "It wasn't? Then tell me what it was like, *Moriah*."

Cringing at the way he stressed her name, she wiped her eyes and nose with the back of her hand, wishing there was a box of tissues nearby. As if he'd read her mind, KC stalked into the bathroom, returned with a box, and handed it to her. She pulled out several tissues and blew her nose while he waited impatiently for her answer.

"A-at first, I didn't trust you, not fully. But the more we spent time together, and the more we got to know each other, I realized you were a really nice guy. And, I swear, when we made love, I completely trusted you."

"But not enough to tell me the fucking truth? You have a funny definition of trust."

KC stormed out of the room, and Moriah burst into tears again, burying her face into a pillow so he wouldn't hear. But he did hear. It tore at his heart to hear her crying, but as much as he wanted to go in and comfort her, he resisted the urge. He made his way out the back door of the cottage and didn't bother to speak to his uncle sitting on the porch. Instead, he descended the stairs and strode purposely toward the beach. Wisely, the old man didn't try to stop him.

As soon as his feet hit the sand, he began to run. It always cleared his mind, and so he ran until exhaustion finally hit him, miles down the beach, and he collapsed onto his back in the sand, trying to catch his breath.

How could he have been so fucking stupid? He was usually discerning when it came to people lying to him. It was part of his military interrogation training. Trust the wrong person and you could easily wind up dead. But maybe, this time, he hadn't wanted to see that Moriah wasn't telling the truth. Why? Because he had wanted her from almost the minute he saw her, and he'd been thinking with the wrong fucking head. And then, after they had sex the first time, he let wanting more skew his thinking.

Oh, fuck! KC sat up with a start.

No! No! No! It couldn't be!

But it was.

Damn it!

Somewhere in the past week or so, he had fallen in love with her.

Head-over-heels in love, you dumb fuck!

The thought slammed into him with the force of a freight train. That's why he didn't want to see through her flimsy story, and that's why it hurt so fucking much to find out she lied to him.

Now what?

Instead of the horned devil on his shoulder, this time, it

was an angel dressed only in a white T-shirt, which came down to the top of her shapely legs.

Now you do what you have to in order to keep her safe. Once that's been taken care of, then you can figure out what to do next. First, save the girl . . . no . . . first save the woman *you love.*

Chapter 18

Long after she had cried herself dry, Moriah stood to pack the knapsack she had used on the run these past few months. She wasn't going to take off yet, but it was obvious when this was over, KC wouldn't want anything to do with her—not that she could blame him. After all, she was just a woman he had sex with and who had lied to him. What man in his right mind would stick around? She would be on her own again, and her heart clenched at the thought.

Taking a few things from the dresser, she spun around and was startled to see KC standing in the doorway, leaning against the jamb with his arms crossed. He'd showered after his run and now wore cargo shorts and a gray T-shirt. His face was no longer hard, but his lean body was still tense. How she yearned to run her hands over every one of his muscles and soothe them. But that was no longer possible. He would surely shove her away.

"Going somewhere?"

She shook her head and stepped over to the bed, putting the clothes into her bag. "Not yet."

KC didn't move from the doorway, but when she glanced at him, he raised his eyebrows in a silent question.

"Whether you help me or not, eventually, I'll be leaving. I'll either be arrested or running for my life again."

There was a moment of silence as they stared at each other. KC bit his lip and dropped his gaze to his feet. Inhaling deeply through his nose, he then exhaled with a drawn-out release as if weighing his words. "There is another possible result you didn't mention. Maybe we'll solve this, and you'll be free."

"Maybe." She couldn't tell him she wasn't as optimistic as he seemed to be. Sighing, she returned to her packing.

"You're still leaving, though?"

"Yes. I think it's for the best if I do."

KC's eyes flared, but he remained silent. She grabbed a few items from the vanity and tossed them into the knapsack, unable to look at him. "I'm sorry I didn't tell you the truth after we made . . . had sex." She couldn't use the word love. He didn't love her and never would. Not after all this. "I was scared you wouldn't believe me."

"I understand."

Shocked, she froze and then turned slowly to face him. "You do?"

"Sure. I mean, what? We've only known each other for a week, right? I guess I would have done the same thing in your shoes." He shrugged his shoulders as if it was nothing. For the first time since he'd found the duffel bag full of money, he appeared to relax. "Listen, I'll help you in any way I can as long as you're upfront with me about everything from now on."

She nodded and twisted her hands together—he may be relaxed, however, she was far from it. "I should never have gotten you involved in this, but when you offered to help me learn how to defend myself, it seemed like a good idea."

"It *was* a good idea. You can't handle this alone, but some-how, we'll figure a way out of it." Stepping into the room, he quietly shut the door behind him. "Look, I'm sorry I yelled at you before. You were just protecting yourself, and I shouldn't be mad about that."

With the door closed, the room seemed to grow smaller as his large frame took up a lot of space. Suddenly nervous, she started to unpack and repack the bag with no rhyme or reason. "N-no, I'm sorry. I never intended to get involved with you, but after we had sex, or even before, I-I should have told you the truth. It's all my fault."

"Look at me, Moriah," KC whispered. She had no idea how he'd moved five feet closer without her realizing it, but when she turned, there were mere inches between them. Her eyes met his, and her knees went weak at the desire she saw there. "How about we agree that we were both wrong and call a truce?"

She licked her lips and watched the heat in his gaze increase as it followed the movement. After a moment, she nodded, her voice thick and husky as she responded, "Truce."

She obviously didn't love him, or else it wouldn't be so easy to walk away. Well, he wasn't about to beg her to stay. It would have to be her decision, but right now, she had more to deal with than the fact that he had fallen in love with her—information he decided he should keep to himself for a little while. For now, he just wanted to hold her . . . no, that wasn't enough.

Before she could react, KC grabbed her hips and pulled her to him, getting rid of the last few inches between them. One hand snaked around to her ass to hold her tight against his groin, and the other went to the back of her head. His mouth crushed down on hers, and although he knew he was far from being gentle, he didn't care. Especially when she parted her lips, inviting him in. Their tongues danced around each other as her arms inched up to wrap around his neck.

Shit! He had to be crazy, but all he could think of was how much he wanted to fuck her senseless . . . to sear himself into her memory, so when this was all over, she would never leave him. Her body already belonged to him, but he wanted more than that . . . he wanted her mind, heart, and soul and wouldn't settle for anything less.

A soft knock at the door had them jumping apart. His chest heaving, it took KC a moment to recover, and he had to clear his voice before he could speak. "What is it?"

Dan didn't open the door. Instead, he just raised his voice. "I don't know if anyone is hungry, but I made some grilled cheese and tomato soup for an early dinner. Brian should be back soon—he called when he left the station ten minutes ago."

"Thanks, Uncle Dan. We'll be right out." Turning back to Moriah, his gaze took in her hair he'd tousled, her swollen red lips, and the passion burning in her eyes. It was far better than the look of fear and regret which had been there earlier. Knowing there was no way they could continue with what they'd started with his uncle waiting for them, he leaned over and kissed her forehead before stepping back. "We should eat. You haven't had anything all day, and you need to keep up your strength."

Although clearly unenthusiastic at the thought of eating, Moriah nodded, silently agreeing with him. Taking her hand, he led her out to the living room as Dan exited the kitchen, carrying a tray laden with mugs of soup and a plate piled high with halves of grilled cheese sandwiches, hot and gooey. He placed it on the coffee table, then handed her one of the steaming mugs after she sat on the sofa.

The older man's sympathy was evident in his soft brown eyes. "I figured comfort food was the best since I didn't think you were in the mood for a fancy meal."

She gave him a grateful smile. He was such a nice man, and she had a brief thought that she wished her father had been like him. "Thank you, Dan. And thank you for believing in me . . . both of you."

KC grabbed an empty plate from under the sandwiches and add two halves to it, then sat on the couch beside her. "No thanks necessary."

Dan Malone just smiled and patted her hand. "Come on. Eat before it gets cold. What can I get you to drink? I think there's cola, milk, and water."

"Water's fine for me, thank you," Moriah responded, then blew on the surface of the tangy, red soup.

"KC?"

"I'll take a cola, thanks." He gestured for Moriah to take a sip from the mug. "Eat up."

Her smile grew as she gave him a small, sarcastic salute. "Yes, sir!"

The little giggle that erupted from her mouth, along with her teasing, had him grinning and briefly forgetting the danger she was in. "Ah, finally, some respect."

As they finished eating, Brian strode through the back-porch door. KC had been pleased when Moriah had not only finished her soup but had eaten a sandwich as well. While Brian closed the door behind him, all three stood with questioning eyes. Impatient, KC crossed his arms as he stared at his brother. "Well? What did you find out?"

Brian sat in the recliner, and they followed his lead by sitting down again, KC and Moriah on the couch and Dan on the loveseat. "First, I called Sean and brought him up to date. I asked him to use his contacts to make a few discreet inquiries. By the way, he's flying in."

"What?" KC was stunned. "What do you mean he's flying in?"

Shrugging, Brian sat back and put one ankle on the opposite knee. "Sent me a text saying he was boarding a flight. You'll have to ask him when he gets here. Not sure what time he'll be here, but it should be soon."

"Wait a minute," Moriah interrupted and then turned to KC. "What does Sean do? You never told me."

He took her hand in his and squeezed his reassurance that he was on her side. "Sean's with the FBI in Jacksonville, Florida, but he's got contacts all over the U.S. He might be able to find out something we can't."

Moriah nodded, and then her gaze returned to Brian.

"Sean thinks he still has a contact in the DEA in Chicago and was going to try to reach him. That's the first thing. Next, I got a message to call a detective, Frank Parisi, from Chicago PD, on my work voicemail. I called the guy back, and he sounds like a real jackass. He treated me as if I was a sheriff in a small hick town, population fifty."

KC and Dan both grunted because they knew the type.

"Apparently, he received the alert when I ran Moriah's ID, which I had expected." He raised his hand at her panicked expression, halting her from whatever she'd been about to say. "As I said earlier, I told him someone turned in your purse."

Letting out a heavy breath, Moriah's tension eased slightly, and Brian plowed on. "Anyway, I tried to obtain a few details from him, but he just danced around me. He said she wasn't a suspect, but they were curious about the reasons why she disappeared. As a matter of fact, he never mentioned the fact that Moriah might be a victim, too, but seemed confident she'd run away. That in itself makes me suspicious."

Dan leaned forward with his elbows on his knees. "Maybe this detective is the dealer's connection."

"It's possible, but until Sean calls us back, we're still flying blind here."

"Well, speak of the devil."

KC, Moriah, and Brian followed the older man's line of vision to the back door. Sean stood outside, shifting his carry-on luggage and briefcase into one hand to turn the doorknob. KC quickly stepped over and saved him the trouble.

Sean crossed the threshold and set his baggage down before KC grabbed him in a bear hug and slapped his back. "Hey, bro! It's great to see you, but couldn't you have just called with the information?"

Returning the hug, his younger brother laughed. "And let you guys have all the fun? No fucking way."

Stepping away from KC, Sean proceeded to greet Brian and his uncle in the same loving manner. He then stopped in front of the woman standing next to his eldest brother and eyed her face with a professional yet gentle gaze. "You must be Moriah. It's nice to meet you, although I wish it were under better circumstances."

KC knew from Moriah's tentative smile that she was a little overwhelmed by meeting an FBI agent. However, she was polite with her response. "I wish it were, too, but it is nice to meet you."

Sean winked at her, then addressed KC with a frown. "You've gotten yourself involved with some serious shit, brother."

Shaking his head, KC sighed in frustration. "Tell me something we don't already know."

Again, they sat around the coffee table, with Sean joining his uncle on the loveseat. He leaned back, crossed his outstretched legs at the ankles, and relaxed. "Well, according to my Chicago DEA contact, John Samson, this Leo Simmons character is involved with the local drug business and is supplied by one Adrian Hernandez. Simmons is a two-bit dealer, but apparently, Hernandez is the biggest supplier of coke, pot, ecstasy, and whatever else floats your boat in Chicago. He has his hands in a few other venues, too, including prostitution. They've been trying to build a case against him for years and are finally close.

"Now . . . this doesn't leave this room . . ." He waited specifically for Moriah to nod her assent. "The Chicago Police Department may be looking for you in connection with your family's murders. However, the DEA knows differently. One of the people they've been keeping tabs on is Hernandez's right-hand man, Dennis Kellerman. He was seen going into Moriah's building the day of the murders, along with Simmons and two other flunkies. The agents thought nothing of it because they knew Simmons's girlfriend lived there."

"Susan," Moriah murmured, then cleared her throat and spoke louder. "My sister."

Sean nodded. "I'm sorry. Anyway, when these assholes left about a half hour later, they were in a real hurry. Simmons's shirt appeared to be covered in blood, so one agent stayed behind while the other continued the tail. The first agent was about to check things out in the apartment when he saw you enter. He knew you were Susan's sister and waited about fifteen minutes because he didn't want you to know they'd had her under occasional surveillance. He figured whatever happened inside, you would call 9-1-1.

"When he saw you come running back out, obviously upset, he went upstairs and found your family. They must have used silencers because the agents never heard gunshots." Looking somberly at Moriah, he continued. "Agent Samson was very sorry about your family, but the agency had no clue they were in any danger. If they did, they would have protected you and your family. The DEA didn't even know why they were killed. I told Samson about the money and gun—so, it appears that mystery is solved for them."

Moriah's bottom lip and chin quivered. "W-why haven't they arrested Leo and the other men?"

Knowing the unfortunate answer, KC took her hand. "They're low men on the totem pole, sweetheart. The DEA wants Hernandez."

Sean nodded. "That's right."

Confused, she glanced back and forth between the two men. "Then, why doesn't the DEA tell the police what happened?"

"Samson's sure that Hernandez has several contacts in the Chicago PD. At the moment, they're not sure who they can trust."

Her shock was evident on her face and in her tone of voice. "So, no one will be arrested for killing my family, and I have to stay on the run to stay alive?"

The men knew the workings of law enforcement, but as a civilian, it was hard for the woman to comprehend things had to work a certain way to reel in the bigger fish. Sitting forward, Sean spoke in a soothing tone. "I told Samson you were hidden somewhere safe, but I didn't say where you were located. He assured me the case was coming to a head soon, and in addition to the drug arrests, there will be charges in the homicides."

Her shoulders sagged, and when she spoke again, it was so softly that the men had to strain to hear her. "What happened to my family? Where were they taken?"

"They're still at the county morgue. Unfortunately, if no one claims them soon, they'll be buried by the city in a potter's field."

KC's heart and gut squeezed as Moriah sobbed. "I'm their only living relative. My mother was an only child."

Putting his arms around her, he hugged her tightly to his chest. "When this is over, I'll see to it that they receive a proper burial."

"I-I can't ask you to do that," she mumbled into his shoulder as her tears soaked his T-shirt.

"You're not asking. I'm offering. No strings attached."

Biting her lip, she lifted her gaze to his. "Th-thank you."

Brian stood. "So, now what? We just wait?"

The other men reluctantly agreed. "We wait."

Chapter 19

After KC had tucked an exhausted Moriah in her bed and told her he would join her soon, she had immediately fallen into a deep sleep. He stood watching her momentarily from the doorway as her chest rose with every inhalation and fell with every release. She looked so small in the king-size bed, and her dark hair was a sharp contrast to the white pillowcase. He couldn't help but think he had never met a woman who meant this much to him and had never expected to. But they needed to free her from this horrible mess she was in before he told her how he felt. Then, if she was willing, they could decide if what existed between them was something that could last a lifetime. For the first time in his life, he prayed it was.

Closing the bedroom door, he ambled out to the living room, where his brothers and uncle were still seated. They'd spent the rest of the late afternoon and entire evening going over the little intel they had obtained and tried to put together some sort of strategy. Sean would contact Agent Samson again in the morning to check if the man had acquired any further information for them. They also decided Uncle Dan would inform his good friend, Matt Griffin, the local sheriff, of what was happening in his town in case the Malone men needed any additional assistance. Brian advised his uncle that Griffin could call him with any questions. In the meantime, they would keep Moriah safe and hidden in case Brian's phone call to Detective Parisi had raised some red flags.

Leaving for the night, Brian and Dan said their goodbyes with promises to call in the morning. Sean was taking KC's bedroom. No one had batted an eye over the fact that KC would be sleeping with Moriah, and she had been too tired earlier to be embarrassed about it. He planned to stick to her like glue until this was over. The day had taken its toll on her. In telling her story for the first time, the deaths of her family hit her again with full force. She was terrified, but the brothers and their uncle had assured her nothing would happen to her on their watch, and she'd thanked them for their vows of protection.

Before going to bed, KC contacted his team's gadget specialist. Tobias Anderson III, known by his nickname T3, was a genius with anything electronic. The six-foot-five, two-hundred-thirty pound, former Navy football linebacker was intimidating in broad daylight and downright scary in the dark. He had a scar that ran from his left temple down his cheek to the jawline. KC had been on that mission when a terrorist carrying a wicked knife had surprised them and managed to get one connecting swipe before taking a bullet that sent him to Allah. T3 had killed the tango and extracted another wounded teammate, all while his cheekbone protruded through the gaping incision the knife had inflicted. The naval surgeons sutured more than 150 stitches to close the wound. While on some men, the large scar might be a hindrance in the looks department, on T3, it had only increased his sex appeal with the opposite sex. The ladies loved him.

Shortly after KC's call, T3 had driven down to the Malones' beach house with a knapsack full of goodies for the brothers. In addition to silent entry alarms, which could be attached to windows and doors to alert them to intruders, he'd also included several boxes of ammunition for the Glocks both KC and Sean carried. It was enough to take on a small army.

When KC had raised his eyebrows at the stash, his SEAL teammate just held up a hand to halt a verbal question. "Don't ask, don't tell. I could only scrounge up six alarms on short notice but was able to pick up two receivers for you. I hope that'll be enough. If not, I can probably locate a few more in the morning and run them back down."

"No, this should be fine," KC assured him as he glanced around the living room. "The only easy access points are the windows along the deck and the back door, so this will be plenty. The other door leads down to the garage, and you can't help but hear the overhead door roll up."

T3 snorted. "I doubt you're dealing with rocket scientists. They'll take the easy way and probably kick the backdoor in."

KC thanked his teammate as he left and promised to call if he needed any other assistance. Now, before getting some sleep, Sean and KC began the task of attaching the silent alarms to the doors and windows that could easily be breached. They also set up a receiver in each of the bedrooms. With the house as secure as it could be for the night, KC clapped his brother on the shoulder on his way to the hall-way. "Moriah changed the sheets on the bed earlier for you. See you in the morning, bro. And thanks for coming."

Sean let out a soft "Yee-haw," which had KC chuckling all the way to the bedroom. It had been a long time since the brothers had played cowboys and Indians or cops and robbers together, but this was the first time as adults that they were teaming up against a real enemy.

After placing his loaded weapon on the nightstand next to him, within easy reach, KC climbed into bed and stretched out next to Moriah. The silent alarm receiver sat on the dresser, where he could see the flashing red light and hear the low warning alert if it went off. He was still dressed in his jeans but had taken off his T-shirt. He didn't expect any trouble tonight. However, he wanted to be able to move in a hurry if he had to.

Gently, he wrapped one arm around Moriah's torso and brought his leg over her thighs in a protective embrace. He was rewarded as she snuggled closer to him in her sleep. Before he realized it, he succumbed to the darkness himself.

Red. Dark red. Blood . . . on the floor . . . on the walls . . . on the ceiling . . . on her family. Oh, God, no! Mama! Susan! Nicholas! Please, God, no! Run! They're coming! Run!

Moriah awoke on a half-choked scream. KC was instantly alert, scanning the room for a threat, his hand on his weapon. When he was sure it was all clear, he turned toward her to see her sitting up, sweating and breathless.

"N-nightmare," she managed to stutter through gasps of air, sorry she'd awakened him.

His body relaxed, and he returned his gun to the nightstand. Edging closer to her, he wrapped his arms around her waist and kissed her damp forehead.

"It's all right," he murmured as he rocked her. "I've got you. Everything's okay. I'm not going to let anything happen to you."

Swallowing several times, she leaned into his gentle

caresses. He stroked her upper arm with one hand and the sensitive outer swell of her breast with the other. The tension eased from her, and she slowly sagged against his hard body.

Closing her eyes, she concentrated on his touch instead of the horror of her nightmare. She inhaled deeply, his masculine scent soothing yet seductive. Her body began to hum with desire as her breathing became ragged. Tilting her head back, she brushed her lips against his jawline as his coarse nighttime stubble abraded her tender flesh. When his mouth met hers, Moriah kissed him back with fervor. She wanted to cherish every moment with him in case things didn't work out in their favor.

Part of her wanted to run to prevent danger from coming to KC and his family's front door, but the rest of her didn't want to leave the man she was falling in love with.

Her hands roamed over his bare chest, back, and shoulders. God, she wanted to lick him. Taste him. Devour him.

Please, don't stop, she silently begged. *Let me feel you. Please, let me feel alive again.*

The blood pooled to her core, and she moaned with desire. She needed him . . . his comfort . . . his strength. As his lips left her mouth and trailed down to her neck, she whispered, "Make love to me, please. Help me forget the pain."

She didn't have to say it twice. His lips found hers again, and he kissed her with everything in him. His hands gripped the hem of her shirt and slowly dragged it up her body. But Moriah didn't want slow. She wanted . . . needed him fast and hard.

Pushing his hands out of the way, she ripped the shirt over her head and shoved her underwear off with a speed that surprised him. Before he could respond, her hands were at the fly of his jeans, making fast work of the snap and zipper. Within seconds, he was long and stiff in her hands as he pushed his pants to his knees.

He let out a low growl as she pushed on his chest with one hand until he was lying on his back, and she was straddling his thighs. Her other hand stroked his length, and his eyes closed as his hips bucked. Leaning down, she continued torturing him with a steady rhythm while exploring and teasing his upper body with her mouth and tongue. She licked, kissed, and nipped his upper torso, not missing a single inch. KC lay there, letting her take the lead as he knew she needed to right now. She had very little control in her life at the moment, but she had this control over him, at least for a little while.

His fingers caressed her thighs and hips, but then she slid further down on the bed as his hands went to her upper arms and shoulders. She felt him shiver as her tongue darted across his dark nipple before sucking on it. Reveling in the power she had over him, Moriah continued down his taut abdomen. He flinched as she nipped at his oblique muscles and threaded his hand into her silky hair, urging her on.

KC knew she needed absolute control over their lovemaking this time. Her life had spiraled out of control, and he was willing to give her this chance to regain some. He might end up insane from the excruciating torment she was putting him through, but he was a tough guy. He could handle it if he had to. *Holy fuck!* Her tongue circled the head of his penis, and he damn near exploded.

He gasped in near ecstasy and half-heartedly tried to pull her off his dick. "You—you don't need to do this."

"I know I don't, but I want to." Her answer was husky and

seductive, giving him no choice but to lay there as her mouth began a full-fledged assault on his cock and his sanity.

KC tilted his head so he could watch her through half-closed eyelids. Fuck, he had never seen a more erotic sight than this woman taking him into her mouth, her pouty lips encompassing him, her teeth scraping lightly along his length. Her long, silky hair lay across his hips and thighs, tickling his skin. Reaching out, he grasped the top of her head as she bobbed up and down. Her tongue licked the thick vein on the underside of his cock all the way up to the notch just below the tip. Opening wide, she took him all the way to the back of her throat and sucked, making him groan loudly. His hips thrust in time to the pace she'd set again.

Holy fuck, he'd died and gone to heaven. If she kept this up, he wouldn't be responsible for shooting his load down her throat.

Just a few minutes longer.

He could last a few more minutes of this erotic agony. He had convinced himself of that fact a second before her hand gently squeezed his balls, and she increased the pace of fucking him with her mouth. When the tingling started at the base of his spine, he growled, then tightened the grip on her hair and pulled her off him. "Stop! I can't take it anymore. Get up here, you."

Moriah allowed him to tug her upward until she was straddling his hips. He ran his fingers through her folds and found she was drenched with desire and more than ready for him. Grasping his cock, he held himself erect as she lowered herself down onto him. The tip of his cock parted her pussy lips as she eased down his length, her heat almost burning him alive. But it was too slow for him, and he couldn't take it anymore.

He thrust upward while clutching her hips and pulling her down hard until he was buried to the hilt inside her. She gasped as her clit hit his pelvis. Lifting her off him, just high enough to make an impact, he slammed her down repeatedly, setting an intense rhythm that he couldn't slow if his life depended on it. Her inner walls stroked him higher until he felt his balls draw up, ready to explode. Shifting his hand, his thumb stroked her clit, and she flew, taking him with her. Holding himself deep within her, he came in streams as she milked him dry. Biting her lip, she muffled her scream to keep his brother from hearing her broadcast the intense orgasm that was pulsating through her body. As the last of her tremors faded, she fell in a heap across his upper torso with him still inside her.

Lying there on his heaving chest, completely sated, Moriah struggled to regain her breath. She closed her eyes as KC slowly ran his fingers up and down her back. He wanted to fall asleep like this . . . with her body draped across him, and the two of them still joined below. As the orgasmic fog began to clear from his brain, reality gave him a shock.

Holy fuck!

He froze in disbelief, and she sat up to stare at him, her brow furrowed in confusion.

"What's wrong?" she asked, staring at his stunned expression.

"Um, fuck, I'm not sure how to say this . . ." Shit, he was a stupid ass. "But we didn't use a condom."

"Oh, my God!" she yelped as she leaped off him to the other side of the bed. Her eyes were wide in alarm. "I'm sorry! I didn't think."

"That makes two of us. And don't apologize for my stupidity. I'm the one who's supposed to wear the damn thing, so it's my responsibility." Pulling her into his arms, he coaxed her into lying next to him, then touched his lips to the top of her head. "I'm clean, sweetheart. I had my routine blood work for the military a few weeks ago, and it's been quite a while since I've been with anyone else."

She rested her head on his shoulder. "I've always used protection, and it's been a very long time for me too. But what happens if . . . if . . ." She let the end of her thought hang between them.

His fingers lifted her chin until her gaze met his. "If I just got you pregnant, we'll deal with it. I promise. I would never run from my responsibilities."

"I know. I just don't want you to think I did this on purpose."

"I'm more at fault than you are, Moriah. I was obviously thinking with the wrong head." He chuckled and let her go for a moment so he could pull his jeans back up from around his knees. Turning on his side, he settled her into a spooning position, tucking her tight against him. "Think you can get through the rest of the night without any more nightmares."

Moriah nodded, her hair brushing against his cheek. "I think so."

"Good." Relaxing against each other, they both eased back into a satisfying and comfortable sleep.

Chapter 20

Leo Simmons shifted restlessly in the back of the stolen black Ford Explorer. They'd picked it up from one of Hernandez's chop shops before leaving Chicago—this time, they were heading to Elizabeth City, North Carolina. The dashboard VIN had been changed along with the plates, so they shouldn't have any problem in case they were stopped by the police—as long as the cops weren't suspicious of anything and gave the vehicle a closer look. And why should they? Leo and Adrian's two goons in the front seats were just three buddies heading to North Carolina for a little vacation and maybe some fishing at the Outer Banks. He only hoped they caught the "Big One" so Adrian would get off his back. It wasn't his fault Susan's bitch of a sister had taken the gun and money. He just hoped she still had them in her possession. They had been on the road for over four hours, and he was anxious to finish this whole mess to get off Hernandez's shit list.

Back at his girlfriend's apartment, he'd killed her mother first. Before he put a bullet in Susan and her brat, she revealed her sister had taken the bag to work. Then, the sniveling whore had begged for their lives—like he would let her live after all the trouble she'd caused him. Unfortunately, Leo had killed her and the kid before he remembered to ask where her fucking sister worked. Dennis had been so pissed and called him every name in the book before breaking his nose with one punch.

Tossing an empty bottle of Mountain Dew into the rear of the SUV, he kicked the back of the front passenger seat. "How much fucking longer?"

Goon Two, as Leo thought of him, threw a folded-up newspaper in his direction. "About eight more hours. Read the paper—that is if you know how to read."

The two assholes snickered at the lame insult while Leo glowered at the backs of their heads. He wasn't stupid enough to start a fight with them since they both outweighed him by a good fifty pounds—he knew his limits.

Fucking jackasses.

It was after three o'clock in the morning when they finally arrived in Elizabeth City and found a local no-tell motel. At the office, they got the rooms they'd requested— two adjoining, ground-floor units around the back of the bi-level establishment. Goons One and Two took the end room and left Leo the other, which was fine with him. He would rather have made the trip with a few of his own men, but Adrian insisted on sending those two assholes to ensure there were no further screw-ups. Leo figured the best way to get back in favor with the drug lord was to do things his way for now. As long as they got the job done, it didn't matter who did the dirty work with him.

Flopping down on the bed, he used the remote to turn on the television and then shoved another pillow behind his head. Pulling out some rolling papers and a dime bag of primo pot, he quickly made a joint. It would help him get the sleep he needed for a few hours before they went searching for Investigator Malone. Once they found him, they planned on tailing him for a bit, and, hopefully, it wouldn't be long until he led them straight to the fucking bitch and the all-important duffel bag.

Blinking the sleep from her eyes, Moriah awoke in KC's comforting embrace. A glance at the bedside clock told her it was a little after eight in the morning. She rolled over carefully to get a better look at his face without waking him. The penetrating hazel eyes she loved so much were behind closed lids, his long, black lashes fanning across his cheeks. A lock of his dark-brown hair had fallen across his brow, and she fought the urge to brush it back into place. His hair was even longer now than it had been when they'd first met. God, had it just been a week ago? So much had changed since then.

She'd been a *blah* in bed with men before, but now, in KC's arms, she felt sexually powerful with a passion she had never known. And she was one hundred percent positive she was safe with him. No matter what happened from this point on, he would be beside her all the way.

"I love you," she whispered, placing her hand on his chest.

She was startled when his eyes flew open, and he rumbled, "I love you, too, sweetheart."

Staring into his eyes, she knew it was true. She loved him with all her heart, and he loved her in return. Closing the distance between them, she kissed him. No more words were needed as they lost themselves in each other's touch and made love again, blocking out the danger she was in, if only for a short while.

An hour later, they emerged from the bedroom after taking a luxurious and entertaining shower for two. At first, Moriah had been embarrassed when KC had joined her in the small stall. She had never taken a shower with a man before but quickly discovered she never wanted to shower without KC again.

After soaping up her body, he had taken her up against the cool tiled wall as the warm water beat down on them. She had hung on for dear life as he fucked her like a man possessed. When they'd towel each other off afterward, she'd been shocked to see where her nails had made bright red scratch marks across his back. Worried she'd hurt him, an apology had tumbled from her lips, but then giddiness had taken hold of her when he told her he liked the fact she had branded him, even though the marks would eventually fade.

As they walked hand-in-hand to the living room, they found Sean at his computer with a cup of coffee in his hand. "Uncle Dan is on his way with bagels and stuff. He got old man Turner to watch the store for the day and already met with Sheriff Griffin and brought him up to speed on the situation. The sheriff will tell his deputies to keep their eyes out for Illinois plates and anyone who looks out of place wandering around town. He's also assigning an extra deputy to patrol Whisper, just in case, and said to call him if we need anything."

Whisper was part of Dare County, and Sheriff Griffin had lived in the town all his life, so he ensured his hometown was safe and secure. There were always at least two deputies who could be found driving around the tiny town at any given time, and the residents appreciated his efforts to keep them safe.

Brian Malone strolled to his assigned, unmarked car with a black duffel bag containing his personal equipment in one hand and a cup of coffee in the other. After Sean had filled him in with the updated information on the murder of Moriah's family from the DEA, Brian had gone to work a little early this morning and had a meeting with his supervisor. With the DEA's confirmation that Moriah wasn't a suspect and there were dirty cops in the Chicago Police Department, Captain Culpepper agreed it was in the best interest of everyone involved to keep her location a secret. They would follow the DEA's lead for now.

In the meantime, Brian had a few cases of his own he needed to run down a few leads on. Climbing into the unmarked unit, he settled in and pulled out of the parking lot, still mulling over everything that had happened over the past two days.

Shit.

KC had really stepped in it this time. They'd all had their share of problems over the years, but this one was a fucking doozy. And all because of a woman. Go figure. The Malone brothers were notorious chick-magnets, he couldn't deny that. They'd been blessed with their mother's good looks and their father's physique. None of them had lacked dates since their teenage years, but they each had avoided long-lasting attachments and complicated relationships until now.

KC had it bad for Moriah. They may have gotten off to a rocky start, but Brian was convinced if they could clean up this fucking mess she was involved in, the two of them might have a chance.

Despite his worry, Brian couldn't help but like Moriah. He had, at least, found a new respect for her last night. The woman had gone through hell and back and was holding it together like a trooper. She'd provided as much intel as she could on her sister's boyfriend, had asked plenty of questions, and hadn't shirked away from some hard answers. He had to give her credit for her courage.

Making a left turn, he glanced into his rearview mirror. Two cars back, a black SUV made the same turn. It appeared to be the same vehicle that had pulled away from the curb behind him when he'd left the SBI headquarters. Was it his imagination, or was he being followed?

Time to find out.

KC's cell phone rang at the same time his uncle arrived with breakfast, and he answered it as he unlocked the porch door to let Dan and his canine companion in. "Malone."

His brother's terse voice came over the line. "I picked up a fucking tail at the office this morning—a black Explorer with Illinois plates. Three male occupants. I've been taking them on a very dull tour of Dare County. The tags come back to an Andrew Peters of Chicago."

Grabbing a pen and pad from the dining table, KC jotted down the name, plate, and address his brother rattled off. "I'll have Sean call Agent Samson and have him track down the registered owner. In the meantime, make your way over toward the beach house. When you're about five minutes away, give me a heads-up, and we'll meet you in the driveway. I want them to see Moriah and identify her. They won't dare fucking try anything with us surrounding her in broad daylight, especially knowing there's a state investigator present."

"I take it you have a plan."

Not exactly, more like half a plan, which was still developing. "Yup. I'll fill you in when you get here. Don't forget to give us a couple of minute's notice."

"You got it. I'm about a half hour away . . . see you in a bit."

KC hung up the phone and found Dan, Sean, and Moriah staring at him, and he told them about Brian's tail. "As soon as the guys in the Ford have a good view of Moriah, we'll work on moving her from the cottage without them noticing. Uncle Dan, can you hide her at your apartment until this is over?" When the older man rolled his eyes at the stupid question, his nephew continued. "Good. In the meantime, we'll make it seem like everyone else is leaving Moriah and me here alone. Three against one guy and a woman? They'll be cocky enough to try and take us on. They'll wait for dark before attacking, but we'll have a few surprises waiting for them."

Curious and unsure, Moriah asked, "What kind of surprises do you have in mind?"

KC's eyes sparkled with mischief. "The fun and nasty kind."

For the next fifteen minutes, while Moriah and Dan prepared breakfast, the two brothers made themselves busy by making a few phone calls. Sean called Agent Samson and gave him the license tags on the Ford, which had been following Brian. The agent didn't recognize the owner's name as being involved with the drug dealers and would have someone check the guy out for him. He also advised Sean the DEA had just received word of a huge shipment of drugs being brought into Chicago tonight. Apparently, Adrian Hernandez was going to be present, along with several other key players, and the DEA was scrambling to secure search and arrest warrants for the huge bust. He promised to call Sean after all the arrests were made.

In the meantime, KC had been on the phone with T3 arranging a few surprises for their Illinois guests. The man would pack some toys and pick up fellow teammates Troy

"Trouble" Mason and Rigby "Peanut" Banks before returning to Whisper. KC told T3 to pass on to Peanut that he would have to do a little cross-dressing.

Banks was smaller than most SEALs at five foot six and 170 pounds of solid muscle, but he was one of the toughest sons of bitches KC had ever met. Due to his size, though, he was often used as a decoy. Armed with Moriah's description, he would choose a wig and some clothes to play her part.

KC trusted these men with his life, and even more importantly, he trusted them with his woman's life. And Moriah was *definitely* his woman, and after she was safe, he planned on making the title permanent—if she would have him.

His thoughts were interrupted by his cell phone ringing in his hand. Checking the screen, he noted it was Brian calling again. "What's your ETA?"

"Less than five," was the brief response before his brother hung up.

"Showtime, people."

The three Malones escorted Moriah three-quarters of the way down the drive, flanking her so no one could get a clear shot of her. Being a federal agent, Sean had his holstered gun in full view. Jinx trailed behind the group, sniffing the ground. It wasn't long before Brian's unmarked state vehicle pulled up, further blocking any shot but still making sure Moriah could be seen and identified.

Stepping out of the car, he greeted the foursome. "They're about a block and a half behind me."

From where they were standing, Sean was the only one who could observe the vehicle without being obvious. Trusting his brothers to have his back, KC didn't bother to turn in the direction indicated. "We'll just stand here chatting until they decide to do a drive-by."

While they waited, he filled Brian in with the rest of the plan. When they were finished here, Brian and Uncle

Dan would leave. Their uncle would go to his apartment and wait for Moriah's arrival while Brian headed back to work for a few hours before returning. The others would remain in the cottage, awaiting the arrival of KC's teammates. After creating a diversion, they would sneak Moriah out of the area via an ATV on the beach, which T3 was bringing with him. Peanut would enter the same way.

Once Moriah was safely hidden above the hardware store, Sean would make a big production about leaving and then meet up with Brian later on. After leaving Dan's, T3 and Trouble would return to the cottage with the rest of their gear, again from the beach, to help set the trap. From that point, they would just have to wait for the bad guys to walk into it.

As KC finished laying it all out, Sean spoke. "They're making their drive-by."

Everyone acted casual as the Explorer cruised by doing the local 25-miles-per-hour speed limit. Moriah held her breath and forced herself not to glance at the vehicle as it eased past the driveway on the opposite side of the road. When they were certain the occupants had seen her, the Malones broke up the group. Brian and Dan, with Jinx following, headed to their respective vehicles while the others walked up the driveway with Moriah between the two men.

Brian steered his car in the direction the Ford had taken to see if he could find where the out-of-towners were setting up their surveillance. The day was cool and overcast, so few of the locals would be out, and the beach was basically deserted. If any of the men after Moriah were on the beach when it was time to bring in the ATVs, KC would contact Sheriff Griffin and coordinate a visit from the beach patrol to clear the way.

Inside the house, Moriah was trembling as she wrapped her arms around KC's narrow waist. "What do we do now?"

Holding her tightly, he kissed her gently, even though the rage he felt for the men in the SUV was coursing through his veins. "Now, we wait for reinforcements, and then the boys and I get to have some fun."

Chapter 21

Three hours had passed before KC's cell phone rang with the call he'd been waiting for. Pulling it out of the pocket of his cargo shorts, he glanced at the caller ID, then answered it. "T3, talk to me."

"We're a mile up the beach. Ready when you are."

Striding to the windows overlooking the beach, he picked up a pair of high-range binoculars. "Ok, give me a few minutes to clear the way. I'll call you when we're ready to go."

Earlier, they had spotted one of the men from the SUV sitting on the beach, wearing black jeans, boots, and a T-shirt. If he was trying to act as if he belonged, he was failing miserably. His clothes and mannerism screamed, "I'm not from around here, and I'm up to no good."

The other two jackasses were still in the vehicle parked half a block away, on the side of the road, in front of an empty house for sale. From that vantage point, they could only view the front of the cottage and the end of the drive-way, not further up where KC's car was parked. Having changed into jeans, a T-shirt, and a baseball cap, Brian was now two blocks away from them, sitting in his own dark blue Dodge Ram truck.

Bringing up his contact list, KC called the sheriff and asked him to send the beach patrol over to get rid of the guy watching the house from the shoreline. It was a good fifteen minutes before he saw the bright yellow truck with an overhead light bar rolling south across the sand toward their intended target. The sheriff had warned his men to act as if everything was fine, and the only reason they were kicking the guy off the beach was that he was in a private, residential section.

Once KC received the word from Brian all three men were in their vehicle, he contacted his teammates and informed them the coast was clear, literally. "Make it quick," he added and then turned to Moriah. "Are you ready?"

"I guess so."

Even if the quiver in her voice hadn't clued him in, her anxiety was written all over her face. Placing his hands on her shoulder, he looked her straight in the eye. "Everything's going to be okay. The boys and I do stuff like this all the time . . . but usually not here in the good old U.S. of A. Hang tight at Uncle Dan's, and we'll let you know when we have everything wrapped up here. I promise this is all going to work out."

He sent a silent prayer up that it was one promise he didn't have to break.

Drawing her in for one last kiss before she left, he ignored the fact his uncle and brother were in the room and poured all his love into it. Never had he been more confident this was the woman for him, and he would do whatever it took to protect her. Not wanting to let her go but knowing it was necessary to keep her safe, he pulled away from her. He stared into her Caribbean blue eyes and whispered, "I love you."

She smiled. "I love you too. Please be careful."

"I always am," he swore. "Now, wait here until we're ready for you."

Moriah nodded, and he walked out the door to the deck. Spotting two ATVs zooming down the beach, he descended the stairs to the patio below him. The ATVs stopped on the beach side of the dunes, and two figures walked up the path toward him. The first person was T3, dressed in tan cargo shorts and a green long-sleeve T-shirt carrying a large black duffel bag. The second was Rigby Banks wearing gray sweatpants and a black zippered sweatshirt with the hood pulled loosely over his head, effectively hiding his face from anyone looking at him from a distance. He was carrying two duffels.

Both men greeted KC and followed him into the house. T3 shook hands with Sean and then Moriah before dropping his duffel on the dining table to unload it. When KC introduced Peanut to Moriah, the smaller man smiled and spoke with his usual Southern accent. "Nice to meet you, ma'am." He then turned to Sean and held out his hand. "Long time no see, my friend."

Sean took the other man's hand. "It's good to see you, Rigs. We appreciate the help."

"No problem. I'm always up for a dirty, good time."

Moriah's shock was evident when Peanut quickly started shedding his clothes. and then relief appeared on her face when she saw he had shorts and a T-shirt on underneath. He handed her the sweats. "Here, put these on. This is where you become me, and I become you."

At her dubious look, he reached into one of the bags he'd dropped on the floor and pulled out a wig with long, straight auburn hair. It was very close to Moriah's hairstyle, and she laughed. As she was pulling the sweats on over her own clothes, Peanut said, "Don't worry, I brought my own girlie clothes to change into." He grinned wildly as he added, "But I wouldn't mind going through your unmentionables."

She laughed even harder when KC growled from where he stood beside her. "If you do, I'll fucking kill you myself."

When she finished getting dressed, KC pulled the hood over her head and around her face. She stared up at him. "Be careful, please."

He brushed her cheek with his thumb, trying to soothe her worry. "I will. Now, let's get you out of here. Tobi will take you up the beach to his truck and drive you over to Dan's. Stay out of sight until you hear from me."

She nodded, went up on her toes to give him a swift kiss, and then she was out the door with T3 flanking her.

Glancing at Peanut, KC had to laugh. No matter how often he'd seen his teammate in a drag disguise, it still fucking tickled him. By now, the man was used to the razzing he received from the other SEALs and always took it good-naturedly. Dressed in hot pink sweatpants and a zip-up jacket, the SEAL had added a moderately-stuffed push-up bra to give him the figure of a woman.

Striding toward the hallway bathroom, he carried the wig he would expertly apply. When all was said and done, and a big pair of women's sunglasses were added, the man could definitely pass as Moriah when viewed from the back and at a distance. Hopefully, it was all they needed to convince the bad guys Moriah was still at the cottage.

Entering the living room again, Peanut struck a pose and batted his eyes at his teammate as he spoke in a falsetto voice. "See something you like, big boy?"

Frowning, KC narrowed his eyes at the other man. "Knock it off, snookums."

It wasn't long before T3 returned to the cottage, via the beach, with Trouble in tow. They'd hidden the ATVs between the dunes of a currently unoccupied house a few lots north.

Troy "Trouble" Mason was six foot one and tipped the scales at 200 pounds on the nose. The blond-haired, blue-eyed, twenty-seven-year-old was a playboy in both looks and personality and had women of all ages throwing themselves at him everywhere he went. Whenever he was asked how he got his nickname, the explosive's expert would respond, "Because I rain trouble down on the enemy before they ever see us coming."

Once they were all settled in the cottage, KC called the sheriff and asked him to tell the beach patrol unit to leave the area.

Sitting on the sand, Leo kept an eye on the house where they'd seen Moriah with four other men. Knowing one was a cop and seeing another one with a gun in a shoulder holster had been the only thing that had kept him from shooting and killing them all. Well, that and he needed the bitch alive to find out where the bag of money was.

The two goons were sitting back in the truck, watching the house from the road. While he hated the sand getting all over him, it was better than being in a closed space with Goon One farting up a fucking storm.

Movement north of the house caught his eye, and he watched a truck as it approached him, tossing up sand as it drove down the shoreline. When the vehicle stopped next to him, he saw a black shark logo and "Beach Patrol" on the side panels. The occupants were two uniformed men and the driver rolled down his window. "Sorry, sir, but this is a private beach. Someone called the dispatchers to say there was a non-resident sitting out here. You'll have to leave."

Leo stood but didn't approach the truck. Eyeballing the beach house, he asked, "Who called it in?"

"I don't know, sir. The dispatcher didn't pass on that information, but you still have to leave the area. There's a public beach about a half mile south of here you're welcome to enjoy."

"Ok, thanks." He slowly walked back toward the house he'd been sitting behind, two lots down from where his target was. The pathway between the dunes which led to the patio and driveway was the same route he had used to gain entry to the beach. When he reached the dunes, he glanced over his shoulder and was disappointed to notice the patrol had parked their vehicle next to a nearby jetty and appeared to be settling in to eat lunch. Continuing along the path to the home's driveway, he then made his way across the street to the Explorer. Goon One, sitting in the passenger seat, glared at him, as he climbed into the back. "What're you doing back here?"

"Got kicked off the fucking beach by a patrol. Gotta wait for them to finish their lunch and leave before I can go back."

When the man sneered in disgust at him, Leo wished he could put a bullet in the asshole's head. Maybe, when this was all over, he'd do it just for kicks.

An hour after being kicked off the beach, with the beach patrol vehicle gone, their little friend from Chicago had taken up his post again. This time, however, he sat a bit further away on a jetty. Brian called KC to alert him to the fact the other two men had abandoned their surveillance, driven into town, and stopped at the local deli. It wasn't long before they returned with their lunch and parked in the same spot along the roadway.

Now, as T3, Trouble, and Sean waited inside, KC and "Moriah" stepped out onto the porch, careful to remain at an angle so the man on the beach could only see Peanut from behind. They stood close together at the railing for a few minutes and engaged in a meaningless conversation. Sean exited the cottage a few moments later with his carry-on luggage and briefcase, which now contained two communication headsets, and made a show of saying goodbye. As he headed down the stairs toward the street where his rental car sat, KC and Peanut went back into the house. Trouble was observing the man on the beach through the window blinds. "He's making a phone call—probably telling his buddies Moriah and you are still here and are alone now."

As Peanut removed his wig and changed into black tactical clothes, KC sat on the couch and made himself comfortable, despite his desire to get this mess over with. "Great. Sean will circle around and meet up with Brian. If these guys are the idiots I think they are, only two of them will try to get into the house, and one will stay behind in the SUV for a quick getaway. We'll take them down in here, and my brothers will take out the driver. Sheriff Griffin has agreed to keep his patrols off our road, unless there's an emergency. Brian will notify him when the action begins."

The men attached their com-sets to their ears with the small microphones parallel to their cheekbones. They were all ready and, now, just had to wait until dark, and then, hopefully, the bad guys would make their move.

Chapter 22

L eo was so bored he was ready to scream. And while he froze his ass off on the windy beach, Goon Two surveyed the front of the house from the comfort of the warm SUV. Goon One was currently catching some sleep in the passenger seat.

Shivering, he couldn't understand why anyone would want to live by the beach in such a quiet town. It fucking sucked. As soon as they recovered the money and gun, and the bitch was dead, they couldn't get back to Chicago fast enough for him. City life suited him perfectly, where the world was constantly alive and moving. He had only seen a few people walking along the shore earlier, but it appeared to be abandoned now. Nothing happened around here, and the silence was killing him.

Well, something would happen later, he thought, laughing to himself. He was looking forward to killing Moriah's boyfriend she'd been out on the porch with earlier, then having a little fun torturing her. Maybe he'd even screw her before he put a bullet in her brain. She was one smokin' hot chick, and he deserved to enjoy himself for a bit after all the trouble she'd caused him.

Yawning widely, he stood and stretched his arms and legs. The ocean's rhythmic tide was making him sleepy. Rolling his neck and shoulders, he checked the time on his cell and found more time had passed than he had realized. Eleven forty p.m. It was definitely dark enough to stage their attack —the cloudy night would help prevent them from being too visible. Time to go wake up Goon One. His sidekick would wait for them in the car with the engine running, ready to drive off as soon as they jumped back in, hopefully with the bag of money and the gun. *Time to have some fun.*

KC checked the time on the old mantle clock above the fireplace. Trouble had snuck out to the beach as soon as the asshole who'd been watching the house headed to meet his buddies in their truck. He would stay there in case any of the assholes made a run for it in that direction. Another minute ticked by before Brian's voice came through the communication headsets of the three men in the house loud and clear. "Looks like they're getting ready to move. Remember, guys, this is a non-sanctioned op on U.S. soil. Try not to kill anyone."

He didn't have to remind the SEALs. If they wounded or killed one of the suspects, there would be a lengthy inquiry into the incident, not only with the local law enforcement but also with NCIS. To top it off, they'd end up in deep, fucking shit with their commander—of the three, that was actually the worst thing that could happen.

"They're on the move, driving slowly toward the cottage, no headlights." There was a long pause. "Looks like you were right, KC. The driver is staying with the vehicle. The smaller dude from the beach and a bigger guy dressed in all black are heading in. We'll take out the driver on your go."

The men inside the house quickly and silently took up their positions. KC headed into Moriah's bedroom, and T3 entered the other one across the hall. They closed the doors behind them and waited. Peanut folded his small frame into the far corner of the living room behind the recliner, with a black Taser strapped to each leg.

They had thought of making it easier for the suspects by leaving the door unlocked but were afraid it might smell like a trap. After several long minutes, they heard the telltale clinking of glass breaking when one of the small window panes on the door was smashed. The suspects paused, apparently to see if anyone woke up, then a hand reached in and opened the door.

The two men stepped into the small cottage, each armed with a 9mm semi-automatic in one hand and a flashlight in the other. They quickly scanned the interior and, as quietly as possible, made their way toward the bedrooms. Neither man saw the five-foot-six-inch Navy SEAL emerge silently from his hiding spot behind them.

As he took the left, Goon One gestured to the right bedroom door to Leo. They'd probably planned on taking out Moriah's boyfriend first and then forcing her to tell them where the money and incriminating gun were. Both men reached out to open the bedroom doors at the same time, but neither hand made contact with the knobs. Both screamed in shock and pain, then dropped to the floor, their bodies in spasms as fifty-thousand volts of electricity briefly coursed through them. T3 and KC emerged from behind the closed doors, picked up the weapons which had been dropped, and made fast work of securing the suspects' hands behind their backs with flexi-cuffs.

KC activated his microphone so he could update his

brothers. "Both tangos down. You're clear to take out the driver."

His eyes then followed two sets of wires from where they were connected by barbs to the men on the ground to a few feet away, where a grinning Peanut held the Tasers. The smaller man just laughed. "Man, I fucking love these things."

KC was halfway out the door when Sean's voice came over the com-sets. "Suspect secure. Sheriff's Patrol is pulling up."

In a matter of seconds, the threat was over. But was it really? Would the drug lord send someone else after he found out these men had failed? KC hit the speed dial on his cell for his uncle, and the man immediately picked up. "How did it go?"

KC let out a relieved breath. "Three under arrest—no bloodshed."

"Good to hear. Here's Moriah—she's been pacing the floor half the night, driving Jinx crazy."

There was a pause, and then, "KC?"

The last of the tension left his body when he finally heard her sweet but worried voice. "Hi, honey. Everything's okay."

"Oh, thank God. I was so afraid—" She stopped on a sob.

"It's all right. Everyone is fine. Stay at Uncle Dan's until it's all clear to come back, okay?"

"Okay. I love you."

KC ignored his brothers and teammates' knowing smiles as he responded, "I love you too."

From his position up the street, Dennis Kellerman watched all the action. He had known those assholes would fuck up somehow, so he'd grabbed one of his men and followed Leo and the other two without them knowing. He was certain the state investigator had spotted them tailing him, and they were being lured into a trap. Although he knew he was right, Kellerman was still royally pissed. Now, he had to wait until everything calmed down again, then plan his attack and get this shit done right.

Chapter 23

Driving well over the speed limit, KC rushed to his uncle's apartment. He shouldn't have left in the middle of the police investigation, but he had to see for himself that Moriah was safe. If he hadn't been fixated on reaching the woman he loved, he would have spotted the dark sedan following him through town. After pulling his Charger into a parking space in front of the hardware store, he jumped out of the car and unlocked the sidewalk door, which led to the stairs up to Dan's second-floor home. Taking the steps two at a time, he reached the door to the apartment, knocked, and called out, "It's me, open up."

The door flew open, and he caught Moriah as she leaped into his arms. Holding her as close as he possibly could, he kissed her forehead and tried to calm her down. "Shhh. It's okay, baby. Everything is okay. I can't stay long, but I had to make sure you were safe."

"I'm fine now that I know you're okay," she murmured against his collarbone. Turning her face upward, she kissed him with all the relief she felt. A noise behind her reminded her they weren't alone, and she reluctantly ended the kiss and then took a small step backward while still remaining in his arms. "Can I go back with you?"

KC shook his head. "I'll come back for you later after the police take those scumbags away. I don't want you anywhere near them."

She nodded in understanding. His gaze flickered across the room to where his uncle was sitting in his favorite chair with a smug grin on his face. "Thanks, Uncle Dan. I'll be back in a little while."

Dan let out a small laugh. "You better hurry, though. This lady of yours is kicking my butt at Backgammon."

Staring back down at the woman in his arms, KC chuckled. "I'm impressed. Not many people can hold their own against Dan at Backgammon."

She shrugged. "I've always liked the game. A friend's father taught us how to play when I was growing up. I became quite good at it."

"Obviously."

He gave her one more squeeze and a feather-light kiss on the lips before heading back out the door. The sooner they wrapped up the scene back at the beach house, the sooner he could bring her there . . . and into his bed where he wanted to stay for the rest of his time off.

A block away from the hardware store, Kellerman watched as the burly man exited the building, returned to his vehicle, and did a U-turn.

Now, what was he doing above the local hardware store?

When Kellerman had watched all the activity back at the beach house, he'd never spotted his female target. Maybe it was because she wasn't there. Why else would this guy race over here as soon as he got the chance? Kellerman was almost positive what he wanted was on the second floor of the building. Pulling his vehicle into an alley three doors down from the apartment door, he turned off the engine. Before getting out, he addressed the man in the passenger seat. "Let's go do this and then get the hell out of here."

The two climbed out of the car and exited the alley on foot. When they reached the sidewalk, their heads swiveled in every direction as they made sure there were no potential witnesses in the seemingly deserted town as they made their way to the door they wanted. Kellerman expertly picked the lock in under a minute, and they climbed the staircase in stealth.

Inside the apartment, Moriah and Dan were in the middle of another competitive game when Jinx jumped off the new couch and stared at the front door. They were both startled as a deep, menacing growl emanated from the usually docile animal. Dan flew from his chair, yanked open the drawer to a side table, and withdrew his favorite Colt revolver. Shoving the weapon into Moriah's hands, he pushed her toward the bedroom. "Go in there, lock the door, and call 9-1-1."

"But . . . but . . ." she stammered, bewildered.

"Don't argue—just go," he whispered forcefully.

Terrified, Moriah ran to the entrance of the small bedroom. She glanced over her shoulder and saw Dan retrieve a baseball bat from a closet off the kitchenette. She shut the door behind her as quietly as possible and then turned the lock. She went to grab her phone from her pocket but realized she'd left it out in the living room. Scanning the room, she spotted a landline phone on a nightstand next to the far side of the bed. She lunged across the mattress and grabbed the receiver. Her hands were shaking so badly, she had to put the gun down on the bed and hold the phone with both hands, dialing the three-digit emergency number twice before she got it right.

Moriah started crying as soon as an operator answered with a crisp, "9-1-1, what is your emergency?"

Through her tears, she was able to give the information to the man. When he instructed her to keep the line open, she told him she was putting the phone down, so she could hold the gun. She didn't wait for his reply as she dropped the receiver and picked up the weapon in its place. Kneeling with her back against the headboard, she pointed the revolver at the bedroom door, using both hands the way KC had trained her and strained to hear what was happening in the outer room.

Dan stood flush against the wall next to the front door, baseball bat raised and ready to strike. Jinx hadn't moved from the middle of the room but continued his warning growl. The dog began barking furiously as the door was suddenly kicked open. Dan swung the bat with all his might at the man who entered the apartment with a gun in his hand and struck him twice in rapid succession. The first blow was to the raised forearm, forcing the gun from the man's grip. The second strike hit the stunned man in the face, knocking him unconscious as he landed on the floor in the middle of the doorway.

Dan waited a few seconds for another attack, and when none came, he leaned over the body to search for other weapons. That's when he was struck in the temple by a second man, who apparently had remained hidden at the top of the stairs. Dan unceremoniously dropped on top of the other body as Jinx yelped for his fallen master.

Ignoring the unconscious men and the whimpering dog licking its owner's face, Kellerman stepped over the two bodies and scanned the small apartment. Briskly, he strode over to a closed door he assumed led to the bedroom. Trying the knob, he found it locked. He raised his leg and kicked the door open before stepping quickly to the side in case whoever was in there had a weapon. Peering around the door jamb, he laughed out loud when he saw his target sitting on the bed, crying, with a revolver clenched between her two hands. She was shaking so hard it would be impossible for her to shoot straight.

"Come on out, Ms. Jensen. I just want to talk to you."

He waited impatiently, and when she didn't answer him, he sighed dramatically. "You're just making this harder on yourself. All I want is the money and the gun. I get what I want, you get to live."

"You'll never let me live!"

Annoyed, Kellerman raised his gun with its attached silencer. He couldn't afford to kill the bitch, yet—that would have to wait until she told him where the bag was. For now, he would only aim to wound her. Pivoting on his feet, he prepared to enter the room, aiming to hit her in the legs. He never saw the black Labrador stalking him in silence from across the room. As Kellerman lifted his right foot to take a sidestep, the dog lunged and sank his teeth into the man's left thigh.

From her position on the bed, Moriah was shocked when the assailant stumbled into the open doorway, screaming in pain, with a pissed-off Jinx attached to his leg. The man's arms flew wildly as he tried to remain standing against the dog's body weight and thrashing movements. His gun hand clenched, and the weapon fired, the bullet lodging itself harmlessly in the bedroom ceiling.

Moriah knew she only had seconds before he recovered and possibly freed himself from Jinx's jaws. Aiming, she drew in a deep breath, slowly let it out, and squeezed the gun's trigger. The man's head snapped back, and a splash of red sprayed the door jamb. The dog let go as the man fell to the ground, never to move again.

Stunned, Moriah leaped off the bed and stepped over the dead body, trying to avoid the growing pool of blood on the floor.

Jinx had already returned to his master and began licking his face again. Moriah was relieved to hear the older man moan. She sank to her knees, weeping, as she heard the sirens of the approaching sheriff's cars.

Chapter 24

I t was after five thirty in the morning by the time all the suspects had been hauled off to jail, the medical examiner had removed Dennis Kellerman's body, and the local detectives were finally finished interviewing everyone. They would have to go to the station later in the morning to make formal statements. Dan had recovered quickly, refusing to be transported to the hospital, and was now sitting in the recliner at the beach cottage with an ice pack on his bruised temple.

Sean was on the phone with Agent Samson as the rest of the group sat around the living room eating the sandwiches they'd thrown together. Despite the carnage and excitement, everyone was starving and wide awake except Jinx, who snored loudly from his spot in front of the fireplace.

KC stared at the big black dog affectionately and vowed, "I'll never again call him a worthless mutt. He finally proved himself to me, and the first chance I get, I'm going to the butcher and picking out the biggest fucking bone they've got for him."

As the others in the room laughed, he glanced at Moriah,

who was unabashedly sitting on his lap at one end of the couch, as his arms encircled her waist. She was wrapped in one of his aunt's old quilts and had finally stopped shivering. He was so proud of her but knew tonight would create some new nightmares for her, and he planned to hold her through every single one of them.

Ending his phone call, Sean took a seat next to Trouble on the loveseat. "Well, I've got great news. The drug bust went down without a hitch. They caught Hernandez and thirteen other men, six of them high up in the organization, with a tractor-trailer full of drugs. Street value of about ten million."

He paused as several of the other men whistled at the staggering amount. "They also found two CPD patrol officers and Detective Frank Parisi in on the deal and collared them too. The DEA thinks there are a few more connections in the department, and Chicago's Internal Affairs is investigating with them. The DEA was able to pick up Hernandez's book-keeper at his house and confiscated a ton of evidence. Samson said the guy is already begging for a deal. Another peon in the bunch is also singing and told them the gun in Moriah's duffel bag is linked to two other drug-related murders in Chicago. That's why Leo and his friends were so desperate to recover it, in addition to the money. The DEA will send someone down to get them from you, Brian. Oh, and the truck's owner just returned from vacation to find it missing from his driveway, so that's another loose end taken care of."

Wide-eyed at the information, Moriah addressed Sean from her perch on KC's lap. "So, it's over? Really over?"

The FBI agent gave her a broad smile and nodded. "It looks that way. Samson also said your family's homicides will be added to the list of charges at the indictment."

Her eyes filled up with tears which didn't fall this time. "Can you thank him for me, please?"

"No problem—I already did."

Moriah stood and scanned the faces of every man in the room. "And thank you . . . all of you. For some reason, you took a chance believing me and risked your lives for me. In the end, you've given me my life back. And because of you, my family can rest in peace. I will always be grateful to every one of you."

The men just nodded with embarrassed expressions on their faces. Most of them weren't used to being thanked for doing their jobs and didn't know what to say when their efforts were acknowledged.

Yawning, Moriah turned back toward KC. "I think I should go to bed. Otherwise, I'll fall asleep on your lap."

He stood and put his hand on her shoulder, giving it a gentle squeeze. "It's an adrenaline crash. Go ahead—I'll be there in a minute."

Speaking to the group again, she bid them goodnight and trudged down the hallway after receiving a chorus of replies.

KC waited until Moriah entered the bedroom and partially closed the door before eyeing his family and team-mates. "Thanks from me too."

They nodded their heads but didn't give any verbal responses, and he didn't expect any from them. He knew they always had his six, just like he had theirs.

He started down the hallway but stopped short when Peanut said, "You're a lucky man, KC. Just don't forget to invite us to the wedding."

Glancing back over his shoulder, he grinned. "As soon as she says yes."

Moriah was coming out of the bathroom when he stepped into the bedroom and closed the door behind him. He was delighted that she had put on one of his T-shirts to sleep in. Without saying a word, he pulled her to him and then crushed her mouth with his own, kissing her until they were both breathless and weak-kneed.

Leading her to the bed, he gestured for her to sit on the edge of the mattress before he knelt on the floor in front of her and took her hands in his. He didn't waste any breath with a preamble and blurted, "Marry me?"

He knew there was so much hope in his question, and he'd completely taken her off guard. When she simply gaped at him, speechless, he continued, "I have never loved anyone more than I love you. I can't live without you in my life. I want to wake up to you every morning and fall asleep making love to you every night. I want to have a houseful of babies with you and grow old with you. Please say yes."

As tears flowed down her cheeks in steady streams, she dove into his arms, and they both fell to the floor in a pile of entwined limbs. Somewhere, between laughing and crying, she finally managed to say, "yes."

Chapter 25

Four Months Later...

KC and Moriah sat on the patio of the beach house, joined by his brothers, Dan, Bonnie Whitman, and, of course, Jinx. Two weeks after the drug gang had been taken down, Moriah and KC had traveled to Chicago where she gave her testimony to the grand jury. Leo and the three other men had been extradited to Chicago to face federal murder and drug charges. They would eventually face attempted murder charges in North Carolina, but the other case took precedence.

The federal prosecutor had informed KC and Moriah they had so much evidence and people making deals that they probably wouldn't need her to return to testify at the trials. Hernandez and his cohorts would be going away for a very long time.

Before they left Illinois, KC arranged for cremations and a small funeral for Moriah's family, so their remains could be brought back to North Carolina for interment at the local cemetery. During the funeral service, he'd held her tightly as she was finally able to pour out her grief.

They'd sorted through the contents of her apartment, which her landlord had packed and stored in the basement of the building, hoping someone would eventually claim it. Moriah kept everything of sentimental value and her own things, then donated the rest to a local women's shelter.

Six weeks after they'd returned from Chicago, Moriah and KC were married on the beach at sunset in front of a group of forty friends, family, and SEAL teammates. She'd looked stunningly beautiful in a white strapless sheath dress which Bonnie had helped her find in one of the many catalogs the store used and then happily ordered for her.

Foregoing his Navy dress uniform due to the end of June high temperatures and the event being a casual affair, KC had worn tan chinos and a white dress shirt. He was the most handsome man Moriah had ever seen.

Sean and Brian had dressed similarly, and many good-natured arguments had ensued between them as to which one was the best man since the other was serving as the man of honor.

The couple was in the process of purchasing a small house just outside of Little Creek where KC had taken the SEAL Advanced Training Instructor position. Moriah was on her way to finishing her degree and had been hired as a teacher's aide at the Little Creek Elementary School, starting in the fall. She hoped to be hired as a full-time teacher after she received her state certification.

Now, as they enjoyed the warm evening, Dan told them he wanted to plan a family fishing trip. It'd been an annual event until the boys' adult lives had taken over, and he wanted to start the tradition again.

Moriah eyed the older man with curiosity. "Does that include me, even though I've never gone fishing before?"

"Well, you're family now, so, yes, it does."

With that, her grin spread like the Cheshire cat. "Well, this family is going to get bigger pretty soon."

All four Malone men stared at her in confusion. Bonnie smiled, having already guessed the good news.

Moriah's face lit up further when she announced to the clueless dolts, "I'm pregnant!"

The men erupted in a chorus of whoops and hollers while Bonnie yelled congratulations and Jinx joined in, barking up a storm. KC picked Moriah up in his arms and swung her around until they were both dizzy. When he stopped, they gazed at each other and said, "I love you" at the same time. They were too busy kissing and whispering sweet nothings to each other to notice when the others quietly went upstairs, leaving them alone in their joy.

Later that evening, with Jinx by his side, Dan stood on the beach, contemplating the full moon and star-filled sky. Speaking softly, he declared, "One down, Annie, my love. Two more to go."

Continue reading the Malone Brothers series with *Her Sleuth* - Available now!

Preview - Her Sleuth
Malone Brothers Book 2

S unday evening, Sean Malone sat on the back porch of his Uncle Dan's beach house. It was unseasonably warm for late March. The outside thermometer had reached a high of seventy-four degrees earlier in the day. Even now, with the sun almost completely set, it only felt like the low sixties. Still warm enough to sit outside for a little bit longer.

With his feet resting upon another chair, he finished the final chapter of the thriller from one of his favorite authors with the help of the porch light. He'd meant to read it when it was first released, but work had kept him busy over the past year or so, and his downtime had mainly been spent trying to catch up on his sleep. Now, he was two days into his month of accumulated vacation time, and he planned on doing nothing but relaxing before starting his new position at the FBI office in Greenville, North Carolina. That was a little over an hour away from his uncle's cottage in Whisper on the Outer Banks, where he was staying for the next three weeks while his leased apartment was being renovated and updated. The apartment was halfway between Whisper and

Greenville and a bit of a mess at the moment—the previous tenants hadn't been good housekeepers. Sean didn't mind, though, since he had the beach house all to himself. And although he was already missing the warmer Florida weather, he was happy to be near his family again.

He'd put in for a transfer from the Jacksonville, Florida headquarters six months earlier after he found out his eldest brother, KC, and his new wife, Moriah, were expecting a baby. The child, due in three weeks, would be the first Malone of the next generation, and Sean wanted to live near them so he could be a part of his niece or nephew's life.

KC was a SEAL instructor at the Little Creek Navy Base in Virginia, ninety minutes north of Whisper, and Moriah was a substitute teacher at the local elementary school. Their middle brother, Brian, also lived near Whisper in the suburbs of Elizabeth City, North Carolina, where he worked as an investigator for the State Bureau of Investigations.

Dan Malone had raised his three nephews in the tiny beach house after their parents were killed in a plane crash when the boys were teenagers. Since then, they had grown into men and had moved on with their lives, and Dan was now living in an apartment above his hardware store in the middle of the small town. The old man was sentimental and would never sell the little cottage, keeping it so his nephews could use it whenever they wanted.

Sean glanced at his watch. Ten to six. His uncle and Bonnie Whitman were bringing dinner over in a few minutes. He was looking forward to Bonnie's famous beef stew. It wasn't often he had a home-cooked meal anymore, and the woman could cook better than anyone he knew. She had been Dan's wife's best friend since first grade and remained close to the Malone family ever since Dan was widowed at a young age.

"Sean? Are you here?"

He frowned at the strange female voice. It wasn't Bonnie —he didn't know who it was. He stood, stepped over to the porch railing, and looked down. The outside lights bathed the patio and porch in a soft, white glow. He was startled to see a beautiful blonde woman waving up at him. Her long hair was up in a ponytail, but he could tell just by looking that it was soft and silky. The striking, green eyes staring up at him were familiar, but he couldn't recall why.

When he didn't say anything immediately, the woman's mouth widened into the sexiest smile he'd seen in a long time. "You don't remember me, do you?"

"Um, I'm sorry, I don't," he responded in confusion as she climbed the stairs to where he stood.

"I'm Grace Whitman, Bonnie's niece."

Sean's eyes grew wide in shock. "Grace? Holy cow! I'm . . . I'm sorry, I didn't recognize you." Looking her up and down —and definitely liking what he saw—he continued. "Wow! The last time I saw you, I think you were thirteen and still dressing like a tomboy."

"And you were eighteen and running off to join the Army." She walked straight up to him and gave him a friendly hug. His breath caught at the sudden contact. "You look great."

As she stepped back, he gave her another appraising look. "So do you. I mean, look at you! I can't believe you're the same person. I remember you had short hair, skinny knees, and braces."

She grimaced, then smiled wryly. "Yeah, well, I grew up over the past fourteen years."

Boy, has she ever.

He shook his head to clear any potential dirty thoughts about her very adult body. Bonnie was family, which made her niece family too . . . unfortunately. "Not that I'm not glad to see you, but what are you doing here?"

"Aunt Bonnie and Dan told me to meet them here for dinner. Didn't they tell you I was coming?"

He shook his head again, this time in response to her question. "No, they didn't."

"Then that's why you look so shocked." She giggled. "I can't believe how long it's been since I've seen you. Between college and then work, I haven't been down this way often over the past few years, and whenever I did manage to come down, you were never here." She paused, then handed him the bottle of wine she was carrying. "I thought a nice merlot would go great with Aunt Bonnie's stew."

Taking the bottle, he indicated the table he had been sitting at earlier. "I'm sorry, where are my manners? Have a seat. I'll go grab a few glasses and a corkscrew."

He placed the wine on the table and hurried inside, his thoughts completely on the woman sitting on the porch.

Wow! Little Grace Whitman has grown into one hot, gorgeous lady.

He never would have expected that. The last time he saw her, she had been short, flat-chested, and all arms and legs with no hips. A little girl. But time had definitely changed her for the better. Now, fourteen years later, she was about five eight, trim, with curves in all the right places, and all woman.

Sean's adulterated thoughts were interrupted by the sound of car doors slamming. Glancing out the kitchen window, he saw his uncle and Bonnie walking up the driveway. Dan was carrying a large stock pot, while Bonnie held a brown paper bag with a loaf of French bread sticking out the top of it. Leading the way was Dan's rescue dog, a black Labrador mix named Jinx. Grabbing four wine glasses and a corkscrew, Sean headed back out toward the deck.

Dan, Bonnie, and the dog climbed the porch steps, and the younger Malone held the door open for them with his hip since his hands were full. The aroma from the stock pot almost brought him to his knees. It seemed like a lifetime had passed since he'd tasted Bonnie's beef stew—at least three years, he figured.

Bonnie winked at him. "I see our surprise got here before we did."

He winked back. "And a delightful surprise she was. I just wish I'd had a little warning. I'm dressed like a street bum." And he was. He glanced down, suddenly dismayed that he was wearing an old pair of jeans with holes in both knees and a wrinkled, grey T-shirt.

She gave him a quick kiss on his cheek. "Don't worry. You look fine."

Letting the door close behind the couple after they entered the cottage, he strode to where Grace was sitting. He placed the wine glasses on the table and set about opening the bottle. "So, how long are you visiting for?"

"Oh, I'm not visiting." Grace began handing him the glasses one by one to be filled. "My move to Whisper is official as of last week."

"Really? What happened to New York? Aren't your parents still there?"

"My folks retired to Prescott, Arizona, six months ago, but I'm an east-coast girl at heart, so I decided to move down here to be closer to Aunt Bonnie." Taking the last filled glass from Sean, she leaned back in her chair and relaxed. "I'm opening my own physical therapy practice in town, hopefully in two weeks."

"That's right! Bonnie told me a few years ago that you became a physical therapist. You were working for some hospital in New York City, right?" He took the chair next to her and settled in.

"Right. Columbia Presbyterian. I was there for the past four years and got some great experience." She paused and shrugged. "But, I've always wanted to open my own place. When Mom and Dad told me they were moving to Prescott, I decided to open my PT business in Whisper. I looked into it, and there are no physical therapy clinics near here—the closest place is a twenty-minute ride. This way, people don't have to drive that far two or three times a week. I applied for my state license and got it a few months ago."

"Good for you." He held his glass out to her. "Here's to your success."

She clinked her glass with his. "Why, thank you. And from your mouth to God's ear."

"What are we toasting?" They both looked up to see Dan Malone and Jinx walking toward them.

"To Grace's new business," his nephew replied. He handed Dan one of the filled glasses.

"Well, then . . ." Dan raised the glass in a toast. "Here's to Grace. May she be so busy, she has to hire some help."

Grace laughed, and Sean thought he had never heard anything so beautiful. Giving himself a mental shake, he reminded himself this was Bonnie's niece. He had no business thinking of her as anything but . . . damn it.

"The chef sent me out to get you," Dan said. "It's a little too chilly for us old folks to eat out here, so we set the table inside." He grabbed the fourth glass of wine as Sean stood and took the now empty bottle with him. Grace followed, and Sean opened the door for her and his uncle.

Grace grinned at him. "I see all those manners your parents and Dan drilled into you still exist."

He chuckled as he followed her inside. "Not holding a door for your elders or a woman is a mortal sin in Dan's book."

"Damn straight," Dan agreed. Spotting Bonnie coming out of the kitchen, he put the wine glasses on the dining table and ran to relieve her of the large bowl of stew she was carrying. "And not helping a lady in need is another one." He gave Sean a meaningful look. "Now go grab the salad and bread, so Bonnie can relax. She's been slaving over your dinner all day."

Sean gave his uncle a smile and a smart salute. "Yes, sir!"

The women laughed as Dan scowled at him. "Little brat," he scoffed in a tone that was nothing but affectionate for his youngest nephew.

Sean returned with a big bowl of salad and a basket of warm, sliced bread and placed them on the table. Sitting across from Grace, he bowed his head as Dan asked for God's blessing for their meal.

As Jinx snored softly from his spot under Dan's chair, the conversation at dinner consisted mostly of Grace and Sean relating what else had happened in their lives since they'd last seen each other. Sean related how he'd received his master's degree in criminal justice while in the Army. After he was accepted into the FBI academy in Quantico, he put in for and received his honorable discharge. "I've spent my entire career, so far, in Jacksonville, Florida. But I put in for a transfer to be near my new niece or nephew."

Grace nodded as she swallowed a sip of wine. "Dan told me KC got married, and his wife is pregnant. That's great. I can't wait to meet them. I barely knew KC since he was seventeen when you all came to live with Dan, and then he took off for the Navy the following year. Since I was nine then and only here visiting Bonnie during the summers and on holidays, I knew you and Brian better."

Sean thought back to his teenage years. He'd been fourteen, and his brother Brian sixteen, when their parents were suddenly taken away from them. The couple had been flying to Hawaii to celebrate their twentieth anniversary when the plane crashed shortly after takeoff, killing all 194 souls on board. Dan, a widower with no children of his own, had taken the three boys in to finish raising them as his brother and his wife had—with rules, sternness, and much love. He may have been thrown unexpectedly into the role of parent, but Dan Malone had fully accepted the responsibility, and the boys had flourished.

Despite the tragedy in their formative years, the three boys had grown up to be respectable men, each serving in a different military branch. KC had chosen a career in the Navy, and Sean and Brian had both gone into law enforcement after stints in the Army and Air Force, respectively. Their uncle couldn't be prouder of them and always bragged about their accomplishments to anyone willing to listen.

Returning to the present, Sean told Grace, "Well, you'll see KC and Moriah in two weeks for Easter since they're coming here. Bonnie invited us all for dinner—God bless her and her fantastic cooking." He chuckled, giving the older woman a quick look filled with fondness. "You'll see Brian too. He's a detective with the state troopers now and lives near Elizabeth City."

"Good for him," Grace replied, then added enthusiastically, "I can't wait to see him."

Sean silently gritted his teeth. He remembered teasing his older brother when it had been obvious that prepubescent Grace had an enormous crush on Brian. Now, though, the thought of Grace and Brian together bothered the hell out of him. Did she still have an infatuation with the middle Malone brother? He sure as hell hoped not.

The rest of the evening went by quickly but comfortably, and Sean's guests left just after 10:00 p.m. Three hours later, he was sound asleep, having a very erotic dream about a woman who looked, not surprisingly, exactly like Grace Whitman, and she was doing incredible things to him with her mouth and hands. But for some reason, there was an annoying telephone ringing in the background of his dream.

It was making it hard for him to concentrate on what his fantasy woman was doing to him.

His eyes opened, and he realized the ringing was coming from his cell phone on the nightstand beside him. Groaning at the untimely interruption and the fact that he was harder than he had been in a long time, he grabbed the phone and answered it without looking at the caller ID.

"Who the hell is this?" he growled.

There was a pause, and then, "Sean? It's Sheriff Griffin. Sorry to wake you."

"Matt?" He glanced at the bedside clock. One fifteen in the morning. A brush of fear swept over him. "What's wrong? Is it Uncle Dan?"

"No! No! Sorry, didn't mean to scare you," the sheriff apologized. "But I need your professional assistance. Dan told me you were staying at the beach house. I'm out on a homicide, and I think we have a major problem on our hands. I'd appreciate it if you could come to take a look."

Sean sat up, the last of his dream fading quickly from his head. He climbed out of bed. "Where are you?" Whatever Matt needed help with, it didn't sound good. In fact, the man actually sounded scared.

"Do you remember how to get to Red Maple Park?"

"Yeah." He pulled a clean, unripped pair of jeans from the middle dresser drawer.

"Well, when you get here, follow the lights." The sheriff paused again as he cleared his throat. "And Sean?"

"What?"

"I hope you have an empty stomach."

Fuck.

Sleuth is available now!

Also by

Samantha Cole

***Denotes titles/series that are available on select digital sites only. Paperbacks and audiobooks are available on most book sites.

***THE TRIDENT SECURITY SERIES

Leather & Lace

His Angel

Waiting For Him

Not Negotiable: A Novella

Topping The Alpha

Watching From the Shadows

Whiskey Tribute: A Novella

Tickle His Fancy

No Way in Hell: A Steel Corp/Trident Security Crossover (co-authored with J.B. Havens)

Absolving His Sins

Option Number Three: A Novella

Salvaging His Soul

Trident Security Field Manual

Torn In Half: A Novella

***HEELS, RHYMES, & NURSERY CRIMES SERIES

Her Sleuth (Formerly *The Devil's Spare Change*)

LARGO RIDGE SERIES

Cold Feet

ANTELOPE ROCK SERIES

(CO-AUTHORED WITH J.B. HAVENS)

Wannabe in Wyoming

Wistful in Wyoming

AWARD-WINNING STANDALONE BOOKS

The Road to Solace

Scattered Moments in Time: A Collection of Short Stories & More

***THE BID ON LOVE SERIES

(WITH 7 OTHER AUTHORS!)

Going, Going, Gone: Book 2

***THE COLLECTIVE: SEASON TWO

(WITH 7 OTHER AUTHORS!)

Angst: Book 7

***SPECIAL COLLECTIONS

Trident Security Series: Volume I

Trident Security Series: Volume II

Trident Security Series: Volume III

Trident Security Series: Volume IV

Trident Security Series: Volume V

Trident Security Series: Volume VI

About

USA Today Bestselling Author and Award-Winning Author Samantha Cole is a retired policewoman and former paramedic. Using her life experiences and training, she strives to find the perfect mix of suspense and romance for her readers to enjoy.

Awards:

Wannabe in Wyoming (co-authored by J.B. Havens) won the bronze medal in the 2021 Readers' Favorite Awards in the General Romance category.

Scattered Moments in Time, won the gold medal in the 2020 Readers' Favorite Awards in the Fiction Anthology category.

The Road to Solace (formerly *The Friar*), won the silver medal in the 2017 Readers' Favorite Awards in the Contemporary Romance category.

Samantha has over thirty-five books published throughout several different series as well as a few standalone novels. A full list can be found on her website.

Sexy Six-Pack's Sirens Group on Facebook
Website: www.samanthacoleauthor.com
Newsletter: www.smarturl.it/SSPNL

facebook.com/SamanthaColeAuthor

twitter.com/SamanthaCole222

instagram.com/samanthacoleauthor

amazon.com/Samantha-A-Cole/e/B00X53K3X8

bookbub.com/profile/samantha-a-cole

goodreads.com/SamanthaCole

pinterest.com/samanthacoleaut

Printed in Great Britain
by Amazon